I0626293

DIGITAL
DREAMS
& OTHER DISTRACTIONS

KERRY NIETZ

FREEHEADS

To Rex and Helen Nietz
My first readers and supporters.

ALSO BY KERRY NIETZ

FICTION

DarkTrench Saga Novels
A Star Curiously Singing
The Superlative Stream
Freeheads

DarkTrench Shadow Novels
Frayed
Fraught

Peril in Plain Space Novels
Amish Vampires in Space
Amish Zombies from Space
Amish Werewolves of Space

Takamo Universe Novella and Novels
Rhats!
Rhats Too!
Rhataloo

Novels
Mask
Lost Bits

NONFICTION

FoxTales: Behind the Scenes at Fox Software
Faith in Fiction Devotional (contributor)
Get to the Margins (contributor)

ACKNOWLEDGMENTS

To Kirk DouPonce for the artwork that inspired a story, years of friendship, and help with my Halo suit!

To Lisa Godfrees for reading *Dreams* despite early trepidations and for making it better!

To all the fantastic writers and editors that have occasionally coaxed, yet always encouraged, my short story attempts, including Andrew Winch, Avily Jerome, Travis Perry, Danielle Ackley-Mcphail, Randall Ritnour, and Ben Wolf.

And to the Lord for bringing this all together at the perfect time.

CONTENTS

PART ONE
DIGITAL DREAMS

PART ONE

DIGITAL DREAMS

DIGITAL DREAMS

1.

It was almost nightfall when Kate got the call. A new patient, an older gentleman. Looked to be in his final weeks. Did they have room? Could her semi-automated hospice handle one more?

Kate gazed down at the com device that formed the top surface of her desk. "Only one spot left," she said. "But it's a nice one. Big room. Lots of windows."

"That'll be fine," the dispatcher said. "Please have it ready."

Kate's office was located at the focal point of two hallways, just inside the front door. She glanced through her office windows, first at the front door, then down the halls toward the patient rooms. "Will we need family sleeping arrangements?" she asked. "More storage for—"

"No, no," the dispatcher said. "It's only him."

Kate felt a touch of apprehension. "Charity case? We usually keep the large rooms for—"

"Financials provided for," the dispatcher said. "Paid in full."

"In full?" No one paid in full up front. "Special dietary concerns?" she asked. "Special accommodations of any kind?"

"This should be an easy case. Light meal once a day. Comes with his own maintenance and monitoring system."

"Own system?" She checked the hallways again. "Lamb's Keep has a full complement of nursing sentries, able to handle any need. If we—"

"Just have the room ready."

The truck arrived an hour later. It was a large vehicle—seemingly too large for a single patient. Its exterior was painted silver and decorated with government symbols. Stars and circles with official-looking badges and text. An odd assortment. One badge read, "Veteran Affairs."

Was this a soldier then?

Kate wrapped a pale, blue jacket around herself and stepped outside. A breeze brushed her face. It was a cool night, but not uncomfortably so.

Two grey-suited men exited the truck and headed for its rear doors. The nearest—a dark-haired man near her age—flashed Kate a smile and said "Evening!" as he passed. She followed him to the back of the vehicle.

The other man was older, with thinning red hair. "Sorry for the late hour," he said. "Superiors had a hard time deciding on our stop."

"You know how it is," the younger man said. "The more heads that are involved, the harder it is to reach a decision."

Kate nodded. "What can you tell me about the patient?"

"Only to treat him with care," the younger one said. "He's important."

Each man grabbed a door handle, and together they swung open the rear doors.

Nestled within the truck's grey interior was a long, dark container. It was shiny, aside from a few scuffs along its edges. Strange, given that caskets were rarely moved. "I think there's been a mistake," Kate said. "*Lamb's Keep* isn't a funeral home." She nodded toward the building. "We're a hospice. We care for patients before—"

Dark-haired orderly raised a hand. "Oh, he's not dead. Miss...?"

"Kate Holden," she said. "I'm Kate."

"Theodore." He tipped his head, smiling broader, then touched the shoulder of the other man. "And this is Jack."

She nodded once for each of them.

"This is where he belongs," Theodore said. "No mistake."

Jack grabbed the end of the casket and started to pull it out. When it reached the quarter mark—where Kate feared it might tip over—legs unfolded from beneath it. Legs ending in robotic feet.

Kate shivered. Though she was accustomed to synthetics, this felt different. As if the casket might now scurry away like an oversized ant.

Additional legs emerged from the other end. The casket's feet clicked against the pavement as Theodore and Jack maneuvered it from the truck to the front door. Only when they reached the welcome mat inside did the clicking stop.

Her eyes rested on the words over the doorway. *Lamb's Keep: A hospice and a home.*

She shook her head. Her home. What was now entering *her* home?

Ten minutes later, the *casket* was nestled against a wall in Suite C.

C had a wooden floor and walls painted light green. There was a matching green chair, a couch, and a small, round table. The bed had a quilt with a bento box pattern—her favorite design. There was also a mostly ornamental bookshelf in one corner. Few of her guests ever borrowed a book from it, but it added to the room's coziness.

The men waited near the door.

Kate indicated the casket. "Are you going to take him out?" She pointed at the nearby bed. "I may need help getting him to the bed." She smiled briefly. "Otherwise, I'll call a sentry."

"He's better where he is." Theodore indicated the appliance. "That chute is important to him. Part of the package, you might say."

"Chute?" She vaguely remembered a device with that name, but it was from another time. So distant now that it might as well be in one of the room's fantastical books. A world inhabited by zombies and ruled by monsters. Decades ago.

Theodore smiled. "That's what it's called, yeah." He tapped the side of his head. "Helps maintain him somehow." He looked at the chute. "Helps him sleep too, I guess."

She resisted scowling. "Seems wrong. Like he's a..." She shook her head. Glanced at the corner bookshelf. "I can't remember. Something from a story."

Theodore's eyes widened. "What is?"

She smoothed her hair, nervously. "I was never much for stories. My father used to—"

Jack smiled and raised a finger. "She thinks he's a vampire."

Theodore squinted. "A what?"

Jack bared his teeth and pointed to his incisors. "You know. With long teeth. Steals the blood of its victims?"

"Like a mosquito?" Theodore said.

Jack cocked his head. "Sort of." He pointed at the chute. "Vampires sleep in caskets, so..."

Theodore chuckled. "Okay, then. Didn't expect this conversation."

Kate looked between the two men, suddenly embarrassed. "You're laughing at me."

Theodore waved a hand. "No, well...sort of." He smiled. "But with the best of intentions." He bowed his head. "Your patient isn't a vampire. So don't be afraid."

"He has a unique condition," Jack said. "A brain issue that requires extra monitoring. Especially when he's asleep."

"He...deserves the best." Theodore glanced at the chute. "All our deliveries do." He smiled. "We're told your place is the best."

Kate crossed her arms and drifted toward the chute. "What...more do you know about him?"

"Just the delivery guys, sorry," Theodore said. "Anything more will have to come from dispatch."

Jack nodded. "They should send you a packet soon," he said. "Probably right to your com."

Spying her reflection in the chute's surface, she touched it, tentatively. It was surprisingly warm. "I'll be expecting it."

Jack glanced at the wall clock. "We need to get going, sorry. More deliveries to make."

"Your patient should be okay," Theodore said. "Shouldn't need anything."

"I'll have one of the sentries check on him anyway."

"Of course." Theodore backed toward the door. "That's why you're the best."

Jack smiled and waved. "It was nice to meet you, Kate. Have a good evening."

She crossed her arms and nodded. "You too."

2.

Kate turned toward the chute, apprising the scuffs and scratches along its leading edge. No matter what, the container had a history. The damage appeared superficial, but who knew what a bump or excessive jostling could do to sensitive equipment. A self-contained monitoring and maintenance system? Not unheard of. But unusual.

She'd had many of the house's synthetics repaired over the years. Even now, some of them needed adjustment. Only yesterday she'd noticed a head twitch in one of the sentries—the one she thought of as "Sally." It hadn't affected Sally's performance, but—

Kate hadn't gotten the patient's name! How had she forgotten that?

She hurried into the hall and checked the path to the front door. No sign of either man.

Seemed neglectful not to know her new guest's name. What if he woke up? What would she call him?

Dispatch would send more information, Theodore had said. Certainly, the patient's name would be part of that.

She frowned. If he woke, she'd simply need to tell him the truth. A name exchange was a good way to start any relationship, after all. No matter how long or short.

Still, it felt awkward. The mystery.

She heard a beep from the office com unit. Perhaps it was the patient's records coming in?

She went to check.

The call was nothing important. Only a reminder from the local power utility of an upcoming withdrawal from the Keep's account. One of the costs of business. What it took to keep the lights on and the sentries charged.

Afterwards, Kate returned to the new patient's room and gave it a once over. Everything was in place. The bed nicely made. The window blinds adjusted to let a sliver of morning sun inside. The sentries had even placed a bouquet of flowers on the table. A nice touch.

She focused on the casket—no—*chute* again. Even with its scratches and scuffs it reflected the room lights. She wondered what it was like to sleep in such a thing. No doubt quiet. Peaceful, even. She hoped Suite C's new occupant would have a restful evening.

She noticed an odd-looking marking on the front of the chute, just above where the top half could lift away from the bottom.

Was it writing?

She approached the chute. There, carved in the chute's surface, was a series of letters: D, R, F, L, I, T, and I.

No—that wasn't quite right.

Squinting, she leaned closer. There were punctuation marks too. Periods and an exclamation point suggested that the first two letters were initials and the rest...were something else.

D.R. Flit! Was Flit a name? Was that the patient's name?

And D.R.? What did those stand for?

Maybe it was the name of the company that created the chute? But if it was, why would it be carved into the surface?

She didn't know of a company by that name, but there had been many changes in the last few decades. Much growth in the business sector.

She traced the letters with a forefinger. They weren't deep. Just enough to imbue permanence. They looked like they were written by a young person. Maybe even a child.

Graffiti on an elderly person's sleeping device? Who would do such a thing? A grandchild, perhaps?

They said the patient had no surviving family.

So many questions. Would there be time for answers?

She hoped so. "Lights off," she said to the room.

And the room went dark.

Kate's night was restless, filled with stress dreams brought on by the many drains on her time. Most hospices the size of Lamb's Keep were run by a small staff of nurses. Or a company dedicated to health services. Hers was the only fully automated facility in the sector. It made for fewer complications on the employee end, but more strain on the technical end. And machines weren't free.

A haze of fog hovered over her morning routine, with much time spent starting and restarting office tasks. Filing reports, checking house usage rates, and greeting the occasional visitor and directing them on their way.

Thankfully, the sentries could mind the patients without her. She'd never been a real people person. Plus, it didn't pay to connect with the Keep's guests. They usually weren't there for long.

Around eleven o'clock, sentry Fred appeared at her door. He was white in color, with a conical head and two large eyes. His torso was cylindrical, with four narrow arms and two legs. There were five such sentries in the hospice. Enough to have one per guest, if necessary.

Fred's name came from his gait. Occasionally, he would take shorter and quicker steps that reminded her of dancing. It was a quirk of some sort—possibly a malfunction—but it didn't affect his nursing capabilities in the slightest. So, as her robot "dancer," she named him after one she found in the histories: Fred Astaire.

"There's been a change in the new patient's room," Fred said. "I heard a sound and saw a red light appear on the front of the patient's device."

Kate scooted her chair back, preparing to stand. "Is something wrong?"

The sentry's head swiveled. "There were no alarms. But I thought you'd want to know."

"Yes, of course. Follow me to his room, please."

Fifteen seconds later, they were at the door of Suite C. Aside from the chevron of light from the window, the room was still dim. There was a pulsing red light near the top of the chute. Kate called for the lights to be brought up halfway and walked inside. Fred remained near the door.

She walked cautiously toward the chute. "Mr....um...'Flit' is it? The only name I have is 'Flit,' sorry. Your information packet hasn't arrived yet."

The chute shifted slightly. She thought she heard a muffled "thump" too. She glanced at Fred. "Is it possible he needs to get out? Does he need food or water?"

Fred shuffled forward. "That's a 2500 model cinder chute, Director Holden. Fully automated. Able to sustain its occupant in every way."

"But it certainly needs maintenance at times," she said.

Fred's head bobbed up and down. "It's properly supplied and maintained. It could go a week unattended."

Near the blinking light was a small chevron of displays and controls. Why hadn't she seen them earlier? The light seemed to indicate that the chute was stimulating the patient's muscles. A necessity for someone constantly inside a machine. One of the controls said "Legs." Would that bring the chute's creepy legs back to life?

"No, thank you," she said aloud.

"Do you require something, Director?" Fred said.

Kate apologized and shook her head. Another control said "View." She touched it and the top surface of the chute became translucent. Within the chute, seemingly dwarfed by the space, was a diminutive elderly man. His head was hairless, and his skin, at least on his face, was pale and thin. His features were expressionless, but his eyes were open, staring upwards.

She gasped and covered her mouth.

"Director?"

She shook her head again. "It's nothing." She placed a hand on the chute's surface. "Sorry, Mr. Flit," she said. "I was startled."

The patient only stared.

She frowned. "He really isn't well off, is he?"

Fred moved closer. "He's fortunate to have such a device. It's top of the line in every way. Only a special person would have such a thing."

Ignoring the man's eyes, she studied the rest of his face. Small scars on his eyebrow and chin spoke of past injuries. Had he been a soldier once? A thrill seeker? A slave? Any circumstance could've been possible, given his age.

His face didn't seem cruel, though. If she had only one word to describe it, it would be "mischievous."

"Special," she said. "Perhaps. But...he's still stuck inside a machine."

"All of our patients are attached to machines."

"Yes, but not like this."

"He's fine," Fred said. "Only a little disoriented."

"Disoriented?"

Fred bobbed. "Yes, due to his new surroundings."

Kate gave the sentry a puzzled look. "That's an interesting observation. Can he perceive his surroundings?"

"Why would he need to? He has all that's required."

She stared at the synthetic for a moment, then sighed. "Still, it's all new to him, isn't it?" Her eyes swept the room, resting a moment on the bookshelf. "Well, he's one of us now and we're like family, right?" She smiled. "You and Sally and the others."

"Of course, Director."

She pressed the "Light" control again, and the chute went dark. The red LED winked out, as well.

"Looks like it's finished with whatever it was doing."

"The stimulation phase has passed. Nutrition will start momentarily."

Kate nodded, then touched the scratched letters on the chute's surface. "I wish I knew what his name was, though. If they'd just send the—"

"You were correct to call him 'Flit,'" Fred said. "It is only Flit."

"That's what's written there, right, but..." She squinted at Fred. "You act like you're certain."

"I am, Director. Flit is his name. The 'DR' portion is a title. An honorific, in his case."

She glanced between the chute and Fred. "Are you communicating with his machine somehow? Does it have that information?"

Fred's head rotated slightly. "I'm not sure," he said.

"Well, what—"

"Mr. Flit is concerned with many things. He's tired, hungry...and alone."

Kate turned to face the sentry. "How would you know that?"

"Impressions," Fred said. "Can't you sense them too?"

Kate gave Fred a confused look. "No, I..." Was this another sentry glitch? "When was the last time we had you verified? I don't recall."

"My systems were fully verified the tenth of last month."

Only a few weeks ago. "Okay...well, I hope Mr. Flit knows that we'll take good care of him. That we'll try our best."

"He understands and is grateful."

Kate studied Fred for a long moment. Should she take the sentry out of service? Mental failings were rare but could prove dangerous. People had been harmed by malfunctions in the past. Hadn't a service unit dropped two people out a window a few weeks back? And last spring a family had died in a fire that their food preparation unit had seemingly started. Both events were being investigated.

The cost of fixing sentries could be high, though. Mental failing often meant replacement of whole systems.

Plus, she really needed Fred's help. "You have a self-diagnostic, right?"

"Yes. Would you like me to engage it?"

"Yes," she said. "Just in case."

Fred bobbed his head, then shifted so he was looking away. After a few seconds, he looked at her again. "I'm operating as designed."

"That was quick."

"You would prefer it take longer?"

Kate heard the clicking cadence of another synthetic and turned just as Sally reached the doorway. "Yes, Sally? What is it?"

"I'm sorry." Sally took a small step backward. "Am I interrupting, Kate?"

Kate shook her head. "It's fine. What do you need?"

The sentry's head twitched. "I'm here to remind you of your meeting with the Daniels family," she said. "They're waiting in their father's room."

"Right. I almost forgot. Thank you."

Sally's head twitched again. "Of course, Kate." She backed into the hallway. Out of sight.

Kate looked at Fred. "You're certain everything is all right here?"

Fred's upper arms flared. "Yes, but I will continue to monitor Mr. Flit throughout the day."

"Very good. Thank you."

Kate hurried from the room.

3.

The meeting with the Daniels was difficult. A mix of concern for their father's care and the cost of a prolonged stay. Kate found it draining. Human interaction always was.

An afternoon of office tasks followed. Bills and government forms. She also contacted patient dispatch again. She needed more information on Mr. Flit. How old was he? How had he gotten into his current state? What had he done in his former life? Dispatch promised to send whatever they had. Every question wouldn't be answered, of course, but anything would help.

Could this chute system keep him alive indefinitely? No one had mentioned his expected length of stay. She'd never kick someone out, of course, but...the Keep had a tight budget, surviving mainly from the infusion of new patients.

She hated the financials. Didn't like much of what she did, to be honest. But the Keep was the one tangible thing her parents left her. Strange that a gain had put her in a position of continual losses.

Her favorite part of the Keep was the portion she called home. A cozy one-bedroom apartment styled perfectly to her taste. Warm colors and a simple, almost intimate, floorplan. It suited her so well, in fact, that she could sleep anywhere in it.

Consequently, she wasn't alarmed to find herself nestled in the living room couch when she awoke the next morning. The lighted clock on the wall said it was four in the morning. That was a bit of a surprise. She rarely got up early. She thought she'd heard an engine roar, though, or possibly thunder. Some loud sound. A noise from outside.

There was a sense of something in the room too. A heaviness.

Squinting, she scanned the room from her position on the couch. The lights were dim, presumably because the apartment's AI had turned them down when it sensed her asleep. There was only the glow of the clock, a handful of lights sprinkled near where the entertainment center was positioned, and the dim, blue security light in the kitchen behind her.

"Hello?" she said, not expecting an answer.

There was silence for a few seconds, then a low rumble like a rocket's launch or an ocean wave. It quieted, then repeated more loudly. Another wave crashing.

The silhouettes of known objects became indistinct, but the entertainment lights seemed to grow brighter. Like tiny stars.

Kate rubbed her eyes and sat up. The sound repeated and the lights seemed to wink at her. Was she sick?

She called for the overhead lights, but nothing happened. She repeated the command.

Silence returned.

She stood and looked around. "Is anyone here? Fred? Sally? Dante?"

"How can I help you, Kate?" The warm voice of the apartment AI.

"Bring the lights up, please."

A sunny glow revealed the apartment's dark wood floor and beige walls. The brown, leather seats and matching couch. An entertainment center, barely visible within a wooden cabinet.

No strange sounds. No unusual lights. Nothing out of the ordinary.

She rubbed her face and shook her head. "Dreaming," she said. "I must have been."

And it was still early. Not even six!

She shuffled to the kitchen for a cup of water then went to her bedroom.

It took more than twenty minutes to find sleep again, though. She kept waiting for the ocean's roar.

Sally was standing near the office door when Kate arrived that morning. The sentry's head twitched twice before Kate was close enough to talk.

Sally raised one of her top appendages, mimicking a wave. "Sad news, Director," Sally said. "The patient in Suite D passed during the night."

Kate nodded. "Mrs. Radcliff, was it?" She opened the door and rested a hand on the doorframe.

"Yes. Not unexpected, though I thought she might hold out for another day."

Another nod. "And the family...?"

"Has been notified. Some came earlier and collected her things. A transport will be sent for her body."

Kate tightened her grip on the doorframe before glancing inside at her desk. Nearly every centimeter was covered by a report needing her attention. Even the photo of her deceased parents was obscured. "I should go by the room."

"Your signoff is necessary, Director."

Kate grabbed her coffee cup from her desk. "I'll go there now."

Suite D was a smaller room, but similar in many respects to C, with a small table, guest chairs, and a window with blinds. The principal color was light blue, though.

Mrs. Radcliff was on the bed amidst a web of diagnostic and assistance appliances. So many that her face was difficult to see.

Fred was near the head of the bed, with parts of two such appliances in hand. At the sound of Kate's approach, he turned and raised his upper arms. "Good morning, Director."

Kate moved closer. "You have the final readings?"

"All scanned and accounted for. Cause of death, respiratory failure. Not uncommon for someone in her condition." Fred looked toward the patient and brought his lower hands together. "I believe it was a peaceful passing."

Kate nodded slowly. "How long until she's ready?"

"Approximately fifteen minutes. I will need to exit the room twice during the teardown process."

"Do you need help?"

Fred's head swiveled back and forth. "I'm fully capable. At peak efficiency today."

"Okay..." Kate gave the room a once over. Aside from a little clutter on the table and a full trash can, the room was in good condition. After cleaning and disinfecting, it could quickly be made ready for whomever came next.

A dead body came with its own time limit, though. "I'll get Lucille to assist you," Kate said. "So we can move quickly."

"Lucille is attending to the bed in Suite A," Fred said. "Fully occupied."

"Well, maybe Dante or—"

Fred's arms moved rapidly over the bed, detaching cables and readout tablets before neatly securing them. "Everything will be ready in time, Director."

Kate took a deep breath and let it out. "You may not be the quickest on your feet but—"

Fred paused, stepped away from the bed, and performed a fluttering series of dance steps that any performer would be proud of. A mixture of tap and jazz.

"What was...?" She squinted at him. "That was unexpected."

Fred nodded and returned to the bed. "Thank you, Director."

She almost smiled. "Did a service man stop by? I didn't—"

"I don't recall seeing one."

She pointed at his legs. "But you—"

"Everything clicked back into place following my last charge cycle," Fred said.

She looked at his lower body. His legs seemed perfectly posed. Slightly bent at the knee joint, but otherwise completely straight. Not favoring either side. Some synthetics were self-repairing, but none of her sentries were. She had documentation somewhere that she could check to make sure. If she had time.

She was no technician.

"So you're okay here?" Kate said.

"Of course. I will handle it."

Kate glanced at the bed again. Mrs. Radcliff's face was visible now. Not that much older than Kate was. Only a few wrinkles on a pale face. She looked peaceful, thankfully.

"I'll make the rest of my rounds then." Kate smiled. "Glad you're feeling better."

"Never better, in fact."

She nodded, stepped toward the door, then paused. "Is Mr. Flit—?"

"Still sufficiently cared for. I checked early this morning."

"Okay. Good. I don't need to check on him, then."

"You do not."

She nodded again. She felt a tinge of relief at not having to visit the man-in-a-casket. There was nothing fearful about him, of course. Nothing threatening in any way. And yet—

"Director?" Fred said.

"Yes?"

14

"You appeared stalled," Fred said. "As if you might need a nudge."

She raised her empty cup. "Still haven't had my coffee." She waved and went on her way.

4.

Mr. Flit's dispatch report arrived that afternoon. She opened it as soon as her system recognized its arrival.

Her patient had been commended multiple times in his youth. Once for a role in the Silent War near the turn of the century and later for an unspecified service to his country.

They weren't military commendations, though. There was no indication that Flit had been a soldier. In fact, many of the details of his life seemed vague. There was no discussion of friends, family, or other connections.

Much had been lost by the wars, of course. Many in the older generations had missing records. Lost connections. There had been a time when giant robots had roamed the Earth and whole countries had been laid desolate. How had anything survived that?

There was some medical information, at least. Mr. Flit suffered from a degenerative brain condition, thought to have been induced by questionable experiments in his childhood. He had suffered blackouts and catatonia his whole life. His last residence was in one of the country's tropical sectors. Near the ocean.

He was more than a hundred years old.

Mr. Flit had seen a lot of life. How much of it had been within the chute? She hoped not much.

Unless, of course, he'd been a killer—or a mind controller. She knew that thought manipulation had been common once. Large segments of the population were forced to obey or have their brains emptied. People died in agonizing and painful ways.

Her desk chimed twice. Once for Sally in Suite A. The patient there needed more painkillers and Sally was unable to administer them.

The second chime was from Ted-someone. An invitation to lunch. She read the note twice before she realized "Ted" was the "Theodore" from the delivery truck.

Was he asking her on a date?

That had to be unethical. Contacting the manager of a delivery stop? Someone you just met?

She couldn't help but smile, though. Theodore—Ted—wasn't unattractive. She shook her head and put the message away.

Now, to check on Sally.

Sally's situation took two hours to diagnose. It revealed a problem with the *Keep's* medicinal dispensing platform—one Kate was forced to contact service for. Thankfully, the platform was under warranty. No cost to her for an updated platform to be sent. A technician would be available too, if necessary. That was a relief, though every update seemed to come with its own glitches. Never dangerous, but worrisome.

On her way back to her office, Kate happened across the sentry she called "Squeaky." He was positioned near the wall at the far end of one of the main hallways. The wall, which had been an off-white color before, now boasted a two-meter-high mural. Squeaky, with paintbrushes in all four of his arms, was the obvious culprit.

Kate didn't know what to say. She only circled behind the sentry and took in the entirety of his work.

The painting was colorful, and strikingly precise. It depicted an ocean scene, set near a tropical island. The sun was rising—or possibly setting—behind the island. The sky was a brilliant mix of reds and oranges. The ocean was calm, with only a few small waves. A solitary whale breached into the sky.

The scene would've been astounding even if Squeaky had stopped there. But the sentry had added another layer—that of the undersea world. Below, two more whales cavorted, along with a bright red sea turtle and a variety of tropical fish. Yellows, whites, blues, and golds.

She'd seen similar artwork before, though she wasn't sure where. Possibly in a virtual museum. Not like this. Not on the wall of her business.

"What are you doing?" she asked finally.

The sentry lowered his arms and swiveled to look at her.

"I painted the hallway," Squeaky said. "Do you like it?"

She glanced at the wall again. "It's...lovely, but it doesn't belong here."

The sentry indicated the wall. "This area was scheduled to be painted, Director. If you would like me to send you the work prompt, I—"

"I'm sure it was due to be freshened," she said. "But...this..." She noticed a stand of palm trees on the pictured island. And near the top of one tree...a smiling monkey? "I don't know what to think of this."

"Would you like me to freshen the other halls too?" Squeaky asked.

"I'm not sure why you're painting at all. That's not what you're designed for."

Squeaky motioned toward the wall. "I'm able to do it."

She shook her head, torn between telling the sentry to paint the mural over, or keep going. The artistry was that nice.

But the behavior...?

She heard the click-click of sentry motion and saw Fred exiting Suite A. Fred looked her way, waved, then went the other way up the hall.

Walking perfectly. Not a skip, not a slide. Only a steady click, click, click.

"There's a lot of strange here today." She looked at Squeaky. "Was there an update I didn't know about?"

The sentry swiveled her way, producing the low-pitched squeak that had given him his name. "What's that, Director?"

A single drop of paint escaped the paintbrush in Squeaky's lower left hand. It created a small circle of orange on the floor.

"You're making a mess." Kate pointed. "Please get that cleaned up."

Squeaky studied the stain, then bobbed his head. "I will clean it."

"And put all that paint away." She glanced at the mural again. It was stunning, really. How would it look if the sentry painted every wall? "At least, for now."

Squeaky pointed at the bottom of the wall. "I have a little more to add," he said. "The turtle is lacking—"

"Enough, Squeak!"

"Yes, Director." Squeaky placed his brushes into the cans that matched their color. His head lowered and his eyes focused on the floor. "I've disappointed you, haven't I?"

She drew her arms over her chest. "No..." Another glance at the mural. "You've surprised me, is all."

"Do you *like* surprises?"

She narrowed her eyes. "I really don't, no."

Squeaky looked at her. "This won't be easy, then."

"What?"

Squeaky sighed. "I apologize. I will clean up my mess and return to my scheduled chores."

She nodded. "There's more than enough work just meeting our guests' needs." She turned toward her office.

"I thought that was what I was doing."

Kate paused. "What?"

"Meeting needs, Director. That's what I'm doing. Guests need beauty. They desire art."

She touched the side of her neck. "We have a nice atmosphere here already. I've never heard anyone complain."

Squeaky swiveled his head but said nothing.

"Squeak?"

"I will clean my mess." Squeak lifted the cans of paint. "And return to my chores."

5.

An hour later, Kate passed by Suite B and saw Lucy posed near the room's center. Lucy had a duster in her upper right hand and was standing within a bright circle of light. The room lighting wasn't supposed to allow for such a configuration. At least, not to Kate's knowledge.

Kate slowed and entered the room.

The room's occupant, Mr. Gardner, lay on his side in bed so that he faced the illuminated sentry. He was a middle-aged man with dark hair. Dying of cancer, Kate thought. He rarely spoke anymore.

Lucy held the duster to the front of her face, as if speaking into a microphone. "How many sentries does it take to change a light bulb?" she asked.

Mr. Gardner's expression was obscured within a breathing mask, but he grunted, nonetheless.

"None!" Lucy said, raising her arms. "The Keep has no light bulbs!"

Mr. Gardner's body moved with laughter. Laughter ending in a raspy cough.

"Lucy?" Kate said, moving closer to the sentry. "What's going on here?"

Lucy motioned to Kate. "Ah, my lovely employer. Won't you give her a hand?"

Mr. Gardner struggled, but somehow managed to bring his hands together for an obligatory clap. Then coughed again.

"Why did the chicken cross the hoverlane?" Lucy asked.

Kate walked to stand in front of Lucy. "Lucy?" She remembered the patient then and glanced at him. "I'm sorry, Mr. Gardner. I'm not sure why the synthetic is acting this way."

Mr. Gardner waved a hand. "It's...okay."

"To dry her feathers!" Lucy said, raising her arms again.

Kate scowled. "What?"

"The chicken!" Lucy said. "It would be under the hovering vehicles, and so would—"

"What are you doing here?" Her eyes traveled the room. It appeared to be in good shape. No glaring messes. "What are you *supposed* to be doing here?"

"I'm here for my audience, of course!" Lucy spun in a circle. "Laughter is the best medicine."

Mr. Gardner clapped again.

Kate crossed her arms. "Was it time for Mr. Gardner's medicine? Is that why—?"

"Yes!" Lucy said. "Medicine!"

Feeling herself blush, Kate looked at Mr. Gardner again. "I'm so sorry. This shouldn't be happening. Did the sentry give you your medication?"

Mr. Gardner nodded, then took a deep breath and started to cough. His mask fogged over and splotches of red appeared on it. His coughing grew more intense. There were more splotches.

Oh no...

She looked at Lucy. "Something is wrong," she said. "You need to—"

Lucy surged forward. "Move away from the bed, Director."

One of the monitors above the bed started to flash. Lucy drew closer and manipulated readouts and switches. A second monitor turned red. It showed lines where there used to be peaks and valleys.

Kate brought her hand to her mouth and stepped away. "Is he—?"

She heard the click-click of another sentry and Sally walked into the room, arms splayed in an imploring gesture. "Do you require assistance?"

Kate stepped farther away and motioned with her right hand. "Mr. Gardner is having difficulty."

Sally headbobbed. "I will assist."

Sally joined Lucy near the bed. The sentries became a blur of action over the patient. Little was said, but Kate knew they were communicating. One of the conveniences of the Keep was the synergy of its systems. It reduced her involvement and stress significantly.

It was better for the patients too, of course.

"Is he...going to be all right?" Kate asked.

Sally looked her direction. "Depends on your definition, Director."

Kate realized how out of place her question had been then. None of the people at the Keep were all right. Nor would they ever be. The facility's purpose was to make them comfortable. Not heal them. "I'm...sorry," she found herself saying.

"Perhaps you should return to your office, Director," Lucy said.

"Yes. I agree." Kate took a step towards the door, bringing herself into Lucy's spotlight. She squinted and raised a hand to shield her eyes. "Could you shut this light off, Lucy?"

"It was that way when I arrived," Lucy said.

Kate found the wall controls near the door. She searched for a way to reconfigure the lights but found nothing obvious. How could she not know that?

She heard a series of beeps followed by a steady tone. She glanced at the bed and its monitors. Was Mr. Gardner dead? Did the tone signal his passing?

The sentries were still at work. Whatever needed to be fixed—human or no—they could do it. And that was best. She quietly left the room.

Mr. Gardner passed twenty minutes later.

Kate got Mr. Gardner's report after she returned to her apartment for the night. The data, which she'd read multiple times, said that there'd been little the sentries could have done. Mr. Gardner's organs had shut down, even as he chuckled at Lucy's jokes. It had been his time to go.

They could have put the patient on life support, of course. That technology was readily available. But that wasn't what the Keep was for.

"They aren't here to live indefinitely," Kate's mother had once said. "They are here to die peacefully."

Kate walked through her evening ritual, using the kitchen's automated systems to create an omelet, a slice of toast, and a cup of cinnamon orange tea.

After she ate, she called her childhood friend, Jackie, and caught up on all the news in Jackie's sector, more than a thousand kilometers away. Jackie had married shortly after school. She had three children, a slightly plump husband, and two small dogs. She seemed to have a happy, though highly interruptible, life. Jackie often said how she envied Kate. Yet also always asked whether Kate was seeing anyone.

Jackie really didn't understand Kate's life at all. And if she did, Kate guessed Jackie would no longer envy it.

There was nothing about Kate's life that was enviable, after all. She could barely maintain a business where most of the work was performed by machines!

Nestled in her bed for the night, Kate stared at the ceiling. Despite the late hour, there was a distinct chevron of light coming through the room's two large windows. Most of the chevron was on the ceiling and the wall to her right, indicating a low-lying light source. Possibly a distant city or a rising moon. She studied the windows but could see no obvious source. Only a nebulous glow.

"What's going on with all the sentries?" she said. "Squeaky's painting, Lucy's comedy, Fred's dancing..." Did she need to bring a tech in to check them over?

Service calls made Kate uncomfortable. During the summer there'd been a spat of such calls, for all sorts of in-house systems. Lots of uniformed strangers coming and going, a few of whom were truly strange. One technician always seemed to be staring. Odd little man who hadn't been at the Keep long, thankfully.

Regardless, such visits were an intrusion and rarely went as planned. Plus, service for five sentries? How much would that cost?

She'd take the sentries through self-diagnostics tomorrow. All of them.

She also now needed to fill empty rooms. "Need to keep the beds warm," Dad used to say.

Her work was a study in contrasts. Warmth projected from inanimate objects. A comfortable life amid the specter of death.

The chevron slowly crept across the ceiling. A city wasn't the source then. Must be the moon. Another grey and lifeless place.

She pulled her covers under her chin, rolled onto her side, and attempted to clear her mind. She heard the room's heating appliance snap on and air whisper through its vents. She thought she also heard rain. Storms had been in the forecast for days. Storms and colder temperatures.

Ever since Mr. Flit arrived.

She closed her eyes but could still somehow sense the light's presence. It brightened, swirled left and right, then seemingly shot away.

Kate sat up and looked at the windows. There was nothing there. No light and no light source. She could barely make out the window frames, or the heavy curtains that hung around them.

The flow of air through the vents increased. The sound seeming louder, more pronounced. The curtains moved with the airflow. Had they always done that?

The airflow changed again. Heavy flow and then nothing. On and off. It also got louder and louder. Was the heating unit malfunctioning now?

She glanced at the windows again, then to her right, in the direction of the door. Was she dreaming? This seemed like her room. The surface of the bed felt warm and soft.

The airflow increased until it was more like the ocean's roar. The pounding of surf on sand.

"Lights!" she said, but dark remained. The pounding remained. Her room-sized whirlwind continued.

Seconds ticked by. She called for light again, and this time light appeared—but not her lights. Only pinpricks in the darkness. Dim illuminations spread like fireflies across a distant field. After a few more seconds they intensified and formed patterns. Recognizable figures that she'd seen on summer nights. Constellations like Cygnus, Orion, and Aries. New lights appeared in the spaces between the figures, forming a full starscape. Her room was an arm of the galaxy. Mythical and monstrous.

"What's this?" she screamed. "What's happening?"

"It's beauty," a male voice whispered. "It's wonder."

The back of Kate's neck tensed until it hurt. She wanted to move but couldn't. The blankets felt like shackles. Cold, metal restraints holding her down.

"Who are you?" she said. "What are you doing?"

The room brightened as more stars rushed into its void. Nebulas of gas and dust. Birthplaces of suns.

Her perception shifted and her vision blurred slightly. Her head was contained within a transparent cube now. A rectangle that threatened to cut off her air. Silence the wind.

It was a helmet of some sort. Lifting her hands to touch it, she realized that they had changed too. They were bundled in thick gloves, her arms covered in red cloth.

"A suit?" She stared out at the room. "A *spacesuit*?"

She recognized a dark shape to her left. A narrow, pointed vessel with a tail that flared out in all directions. The ship moved silently across the room then winked out near the door.

"What was that?"

"An old friend," the voice said.

Other objects floated into the room. Swimming amidst the stars and nebula. Mechanical devices unlike anything she'd ever seen. Synthetic constructs shaped like sea animals. Jellyfish and squid. Nautili and scallops. Strange multi-legged creatures. Industrious things. Frightening things.

Kate raised her hands to shield her face. One of the creatures, a squid with a tapered head, noticed her and angled her direction. It moved with an undulating motion. Surge and then pause. Surge and pause.

"What—?"

The squid reached a spot near her head, then darted toward her shoulder. It meandered its way down until it reached her bed, then spun and moved upwards again.

A school of semi-transparent jellyfish formed a sphere-like formation near the window. A nautilus spun past her eyes before jetting away. Two crab creatures slinked sideways near the floor.

"Deep calls to deep," the voice said. "Your waves have rushed over me."

Kate's emotions surged with the sound and the movements of the mechanical creatures. Her fears were pushed back, replaced by wonder. By joy. She attempted to touch the squid, but it alluded her.

"All streams flow to the sea, but the sea is never full."

Her chest was filled with new warmth. Her face tingled inside the helmet. Her eyes were moist and heavy. Her arms drifted upwards. As if she really were in the sea. Would she drown? Would she die now, filled with splendor?

"Incredible," she whispered. "How can this be?"

There was a laugh, and the dream began to fade. The stars, the creatures, and her suit. Finally, the sound—the ocean's roar—began to soften.

"No, wait," she said. "Don't go!"

She stretched and tried to capture anything she could—a creature, a star, even the light itself. But it fell away. All returned to nothing. All was lost.

All became dark.

6.

Her head was foggy the following morning. Everything in her apartment looked normal. Everything functioned as it should. No stars, no floating mechanical sea creatures. No starships. Nothing unusual. Had the night's events been real? They seemed so at the time. But now? She had no clue.

There was a message waiting for her at her office when she arrived. A potential occupant for one of the Keep's rooms. A middle-aged woman dying from a long undiagnosed blood condition. Multiple organs were damaged. A family soon to be left behind. She required the best service possible.

Kate summoned the sentries one by one and had them perform their self-diagnostic procedure. No significant anomalies were found. Even known anomalies—small imperfections like Fred's limp, Sally's head twitch, and Dante's tendency for deliberate speech—had seemingly disappeared.

What was happening here? She knew what she'd observed the day prior. The hall painting. The comedy routine. Those weren't normal sentry behaviors. So where had they come from?

Lucy's routine may have contributed to Mr. Gardner's demise, regardless of what the final report said. How could Kate even know that the results were valid? They'd been crafted by the sentries, after all! What if there was some design flaw in all of them? Someone could get thrown out a window. Or cooked alive!

She made a call to the sentry support group. They promised to send someone over. For a fee, of course. She hoped that their technician wasn't too disruptive. Or expensive.

An hour later, Kate made her usual walk through the facility. Every sentry greeted her as she passed. Every room was in the proper condition. Everything clean. Patients cared for. Everything where it should be.

Eventually, she found herself in Mr. Flit's room. It was dimmer than it should have been, with the window blinds still shut. Why hadn't Fred adjusted the lighting yet?

She manipulated the blinds herself, manually. The room filled with light and color. She brushed her fingertips over the nearby table, detected no dust, and smiled.

She approached Mr. Flit's monitoring device. His chute. There was a single green light on top—a sign, she assumed, that everything was fine. That the technology was performing as it should.

She studied the chute's chevron of controls for a moment. Would it be rude to look in on the occupant? It seemed unnecessarily intrusive. Does anyone like to be watched while they sleep?

Part of her job was observation, though. Observation, verification, and determination. She touched the "View" control and bent over the chute. The person inside was—

Not Mr. Flit!

Gasping, she brought a hand to her mouth and took a couple steps back.

"I need a sentry!" she said to the room. "One of our patients is gone."

The room confirmed her request.

She inched toward the chute again. Who was in there now? The face was young with a full head of dark, wavy hair. Late teens or early twenties, she'd guess. Too young for such a device. Too young for a place like this.

She leaned closer. The man's eyes were closed, but portions of his face now seemed familiar. The angle of his jaw. The shape of his nose and ears, though smaller, were similar too.

Was it Mr. Flit somehow? Still inside the chute, but younger?

Could it—?

She heard the approach of a sentry and felt a surge of relief. If nothing else, the synthetic could help figure this out. They'd have access to internal recordings and measurements. They could tell who was really in the chute. Or if anyone had visited recently.

"You require assistance, Director?" Fred's voice, sounding concerned.

She stepped back and pointed at the chute. "Something happened to the patient."

Fred's head swiveled to look at her. "To Mr. Flit? I was here only twenty minutes ago."

"Yes," she said. "I mean, if that's him. I'm not really sure it is."

Fred approached the chute and interacted with the controls. "Mr. Flit is as he should be," Fred said. "His deterioration continues, but otherwise his systems are—"

"Don't say *normal*, Fred," she said, scowling. "He's *not* normal."

Fred looked at her again. "Well, of course he's not. He's a unique individual, sent here for our specialized attention."

Her face warmed with anger. She pointed at the chute. "Look at him, Fred. What do you see?"

Fred shuffled to the left, and raising his head, peered within. "He appears generally unchanged." He looked her way. "Every human changes daily at the cellular level, but most of those changes are imperceivable to—"

"What's wrong with you!" Kate squeezed next to the sentry and looked inside.

Mr. Flit was back. Old Mr. Flit, just as he'd looked the first time she'd seen him.

Kate shook her head and stepped away. "I'm losing my mind."

"Director?"

She pointed. "It's impossible."

"What is impossible, Kate?"

She closed her hands into fists. "When I looked before, it wasn't him. Not old him, anyway." She searched the floor, studying the patterns in the wood. "It was a younger version. At least...I think it was."

"I don't believe that's true." Fred rested a hand on the chute. "Though it's a marvelous monitor, a cinder chute isn't restorative. It can't turn back time or repair damaged cells." Fred folded all four hands over his chest. "At least, not to my knowledge."

Kate heard the movement of another sentry in the hall behind them. A few seconds later, she heard Lucy's voice. "Do you require additional assistance, Director?"

Kate turned to look at Lucy. "I don't know. I...I don't think so."

Lucy's head slid upward and her eye's widened. "If *you* don't know, who does?"

Kate glanced at the chute. Mr. Flit's right eyebrow—the one with the scar—was higher than the other. As if he too were awaiting a response.

She looked at Fred. "Is the patient listening, Fred? Is he currently involved?"

Now Fred's head slid upward. "Director?"

She pointed at the sentry. "Can he hear what we're saying?"

"I supposed that's possible, but it seems unlikely. The chute is heavily insulated and—"

"You implied that he could communicate before," Kate said. "That you got impressions?"

"Pardon. From Mr. Flit? But he's unconscious."

She felt a sudden urge to strangle the sentry. "He was unconscious when he was admitted!" she said. "And you said you could talk to him."

Fred looked at Lucy, then raised his upper arms to approximate a shrug. "I have no recollection of that discussion. Are you sure it was me?"

She glanced at Mr. Flit's face again. It was stoic now. As composed as a cadaver in a real casket. She touched the control to make the chute's top opaque, hiding him from view. She got an idea then. A terrible idea. "It *is* him, isn't it?" she said.

"Director?" the sentries said in unison.

"He's one of those..." She brought her hands near her head. "Mind controllers from the past." She paced toward the bookshelf, noting how many of the covers were either white or red. "And now he's doing that here. To me." She turned and pointed at the sentries. "To all of us."

Fred and Lucy exchanged a look.

"I'm not familiar with a mind controller," Lucy said. "Is that a psychological device? One that would help with dementia and other brain anomalies?"

Shaking her head, Kate remembered the message she'd gotten from Theodore. That was a person she could ask. A real person. Someone who might know something.

She pushed past Lucy to the hallway, and turning left, headed toward her office. Ahead and on the left was Dante. He had a reddish tint to his body, which had prompted her to name him what she had. It wasn't quite an "inferno" color, but it was close enough.

Dante raised his upper arms and started to sing. She wasn't sure what the song was because it was in another language. The technique was loud and inflective, though. As if Dante were telling a story. It made Kate think of heavy women and helmets with horns.

She raised a finger to her lips. "Stop that!" she said. "You can't do that here!"

Dante lowered his arms. "I'm merely singing, Director. Signifying joy using—"

26

She placed a hand over his facial speaker. "You're too loud. You'll disturb our guests."

Dante spoke again, so softly that she couldn't understand him.

She removed her hand.

"I apologize, Director. That song needed to be sung. And at that precise volume."

She studied the sentry a second, then pointed toward Flit's room. "Was it him?" she said. "Did he tell you to sing like that?"

Dante looked the way she was pointing. "Who, ma'am?"

"Flit!" she said. "Mr. Flit!"

Dante looked her direction, then crouched and stepped so close his face almost touched hers. "And what if it was, Miss Director? What if it was?"

Kate gasped and stepped away.

Dante made a sound like a chuckle before reverting to his normal stance. "Are you all right, Director?" he said. "Do you require assistance?"

"No...no..." She turned and retreated toward her office. "I'm fine. Go back to your chores." She glanced at him. He was still standing naturally. "No more singing, all right?"

Dante raised a hand. "Yes, Kate. No singing. Back to work I go."

7.

She reached her office and shut the door. Through the windows, she made a quick check of the hallways in both directions. All looked calm. No dancing, painting, or singing sentries as far as she could see.

She touched the activation spot on her desk and the built-in communication device flashed to life. A second later, she brought up her message list and started scrolling. Had she kept the contact? She thought she had.

After a few moments' search, she found the message from Ted inviting her to lunch. She retrieved his information and set the com to connect. A swirling pattern filled the screen.

Ten seconds went by. Then twenty.

The swirl dissolved and a man's face appeared. It was Ted, but she almost didn't recognize him. He was wearing a comfortable blue-and-red shirt and his hair seemed wavier somehow. It was like a different person. A more interesting person.

"Hello?" the man said. "Kate, right?"

Feeling her face fill with color, she glanced away from the screen nervously. She saw her coffee cup and decided to use that as a shield.

She brought it to her lips, took a sip, then smiled. "I'm just now getting through my messages, sorry." She motioned to the office behind her. "Always something here."

Ted smiled. "I understand. Been working some long days myself. Guess we have that in common."

She felt the urge to simply chat for a while. To indulge in conversation with someone new. Someone who wasn't dying. But she had a reason for calling. A mission.

"I hope I wasn't too forward in my message," Ted said. "Contacting you out of the blue. I wasn't sure how to—"

Kate fluttered a hand and returned her coffee cup to the desk. "That's fine, really. I need to ask you something."

Ted raised an eyebrow and moved closer on his end. "Sure. What?"

"Remember the patient you brought us? Mister Flit?"

Ted looked upwards as if in thought. "You'll have to refresh my memory. I have a lot of—"

"I'm at Lamb's Keep? You brought us a patient in a...a dark chute. An older gentleman. Very old, actually."

Ted smiled. "Oh sure, how could I forget? He had one of the self-propelled models. The ones with the gangly legs. Makes me think of a headless alpaca."

"An alpaca?"

"You know what those are, right?" He spread his hands apart. "Long necks and legs. Like llamas, but smaller."

She shook her head. "I don't think I do."

Ted's face reddened. "That's all right. I'm full of random facts." He glanced to his right. "What was your question again?"

She nodded. "I got the patient's report from dispatch. It really doesn't give me much, though, and..." She reached for her cup again. "We've been having issues here."

Ted's eyebrows rose again. "With him or his chute? He was comatose, right? Usually that means that they stay—"

"In the chute," she said. "Right. All the time. And everything seems fine with it. But..." She remembered her dream of space and sea. "Something..." She sighed and shook her head. "Everything's not fine."

His face showed concern. "What's going on, Kate?"

She wanted to stand and check the halls again. To make certain the sentries weren't up to no good. Instead, she looked at the picture of her parents on the nearby wall.

What would they do here? Dad would doubtless try to figure it out. Take every sentry apart if he had to. And Mom? Mom would go on like nothing strange had happened.

But would any of this have happened to them? Or were strange occurrences something only she could experience? Was perception the issue? Was it all in her mind?

"Kate?"

She looked at Ted and smiled. "My nights have been a little off. Sorry." She raised her cup. "Need more coffee!"

Ted smiled. Waited.

She took another sip. "Anyway, there have been some oddities here of late."

"What sort of oddities?"

"Strange behavior from the sentries."

"Your synthetic assistants?"

"Correct." She glanced at the picture again. "They help with our guests and perform maintenance. They basically run the place." She forced a smile. "I mean, they've always been a little quirky, but now their quirkiness is off the charts."

Ted squinted. "Sorry to hear that. What are we talking about here?"

"You wouldn't believe me."

Ted chuckled. "I like a good story as much as the next guy."

She suddenly felt anxious. Impatient. "Okay. Fine. Stuff like dancing, singing, and painting."

"Your robots dance?"

"They aren't supposed to. But one of them does now. I don't know why."

Ted chuckled again.

Kate straightened. "Are you laughing at me?"

He raised a hand. "Not at you, no. It's just..." Another smile. "This conversation isn't going the way I expected. You seem to be good at that. Surprising me."

"I'm sorry. I know it's unusual."

"Well, I'll admit that does seem strange. Not sure what it has to do with—"

"Because it started when he *arrived*!" The last word came out a little louder than was necessary. Enough that Ted started.

Kate took a deep breath. Smiled. "Anyway, if you know something, anything that would help, could you—"

"I don't have access to patient information," Ted said. "Not really. I mean, I can ask around...but I'm still only a delivery guy."

"Right. I know. But you're the only real source I have."

He shrugged. "With a lot of the older generation it's hard to know what they went through. I still run across wreckage from the battles. Abandoned shells of old mechanicals. Giant gears and tracks." He shook his head. "Everyone was mind-controlled back then. It was how the tyrants stayed in power."

"Tyrants, right," she blurted out. "I think that's what Mr. Flit was."

"You think he was what?"

"I think he controlled people's minds. I think—"

"The bad guys were dealt with," Ted said. "Everyone knows that."

"Yeah? Well, what if they weren't? What if one of them escaped somehow?"

Ted was silent for a moment. "You think that's what Mr. Flit is. An escaped tyrant?"

She shrugged. "I know it sounds strange," she said. "But is it possible?"

"I don't know..."

"Could you see what you can find out? Please."

Ted contemplated for a few seconds, then bobbed his head once. "Sure, I'll check around. I wouldn't get my hopes up, though."

"I'll accept whatever you find." She smiled and crossed her chest. "I promise."

Ted nodded, then smiled and shook his head. "I was really hoping to—"

"I know," Kate said. "I know what you were hoping." She took a sip of coffee. "But I'm busy here, okay? Like, always busy. I really don't have time for..." She glanced at the windows. "...outside things."

"Hey, I'm not a thing!"

She chuckled. "You know what I mean. Things that take time." Another sip, followed by a *thunk* as she put the cup down on her desk.

Ted looked thoughtful, then frowned and raised a shoulder. "Well, I'm sorry to hear that."

"That's okay. I'm the one who should be sorry. I've gotten so used to..." She shook her head. She was where she was supposed to be. For now, anyway. She smiled. "Anyway, I appreciate whatever you can find. It would help a lot." With a closing nod, she pushed the session away.

What now? She studied her parents' picture then remembered the long list of forms that needed her attention. Exit reports for the patients that had recently passed. Several queries from families wanting to bring their loved ones in. Government and sales inquiries.

She activated her desk again, and sighing, began to work.

8.

30

A couple hours later there was a buzz from the front door. Kate glanced at the clock in the center of her desk. It was well past visiting hours, and she hadn't been notified of any deliveries. There had been a request, of course, but no official word yet.

She thought of Theodore's delivery a week earlier. It had been short notice, but not without *some* notice. She frowned and smoothed her hair.

This wouldn't be him, of course. She felt a twinge of disappointment.

She stood and checked the hallways again. Everything remained calm. No unusual behavior. No unusual sounds. Good.

There was another buzz followed by a heavy bang on the front door. She startled then scrambled to the door. She checked the security peephole and saw a solitary person with a thin blue coat and matching cap. The cap bore an insignia that read "SenTech."

She pulled open the door. "Hello, are you--?"

There was a burst of cold and a swirl of snow. She had only a second to size the person up—a middle-aged man in dark blue overalls—before he stepped, somewhat forcefully, inside. He seemed to notice her discomfort because he removed his hat—revealing thick, dark hair—and dipped his head. "Sorry, ma'am, it's really cold out there." He showed her reddened hands. "Left my gloves in the *huve*." He smiled. "Without them I'm little good to anyone."

"So, you're here to—?"

He dipped his head again. "Dean of SenTech, yes. You called about sentry misbehavior?"

"Dean of Sen—?" She thought for a moment. "Oh yes," she said. "I guess I did. Sorry."

Dean brushed past her to the second set of doors and walked through them to the foyer. He put his hands on his hips and looked down both hallways as if sizing up a buffet.

Kate entered behind him. Though shorter than her, Dean the repairman seemed much larger. Like he occupied more space than he should.

He scratched his head and replaced his hat. "So, where are they now?" he asked.

"Spread throughout the facility." She indicated the leftmost hall. "We have five rooms and they—"

He frowned. "Free-rangers, huh? Always complicates things." He waved. "Suppose I should go track them down." He slid a hand into his coat, brought out a square device, and studied its screen.

"That shouldn't be necessary," she said. "I can call them from the front office here."

"Don't bother." He held up the device. "Got my tracker here. I can find them when I need to." His hands returned to his hips and he made another visual sweep of the area. Finally, his gaze returned to her. He seemed to sweep her over too. "Nice place you got here. You the owner?"

She drew her arms over her chest. Nodded.

"Hospice, is it?"

She nodded again. "Yes. Full service."

He raised an eyebrow. "And how many...users you got here now?"

"You mean guests?" she said. "We're down some. Only three."

"Wouldn't want to bother any of them." He nodded. "How about staff?"

Kate felt a twinge of trepidation. "Why is that relevant, Mr....um...Dean?"

"Dean Shuer, actually." He smiled. "Sorry for my nose. Part of being a tech guy. Always want to know it all, even if it isn't directly my business." He raised his device again. "Solving mysteries, after all. I'm like a detective, but more expensive."

Kate's eyes widened.

He looked at her with squinted eyes then chuckled. "Only kidding. I'm as reasonable as they come." He checked his device. "Okay...I'm showing one to the right here." He pivoted slowly. "I'll just wander that way and see what I can see."

"There are guests that way too," she said. "It would be better if I had the sentries come here."

He raised a finger to his lips. "I can be stealthy, Miss Kate. No worries there." He indicated the right hall. "Helps if I observe them in their surroundings."

Another odd sign. "I didn't give you my name," she said.

He pointed at his device. "Have it right here. Dispatch gave it to me." He smiled. "As to your marital status..." He nodded at her. "I didn't see a ring, so I figured." His smile broadened. "Like a detective, see?"

"Maybe I don't wear a ring," she said. "Or I lost it."

He squinted, then shook his head. "Nah, you're not the type. You'd wear a ring if you had one."

Something about this was...off. And a little creepy. But she'd met enough technical people to know that awkwardness wasn't that unusual. Smart with the technology, but with humans...not so much. "I lost my ring."

He laughed and shook his head again. "Don't think you did, Miss Kate." He pointed to the right hallway and took a step. "Anyway, I'll be down there checking your sentries. Let me know if you need anything."

Kate glanced toward the front window. "How bad is it out there?" she asked, hoping to normalize the conversation. "Looks like the weather has taken a turn."

Dean paused midstride. "Bit rough getting up here, sure," he said. "Lots of drifting. Nothing a hover couldn't get through." He smiled. "Afraid I'll get stuck?"

"Well, I'd hate for you to..." She pointed at his device. "I'm sorry. I thought you'd just have a tool to connect to the sentries to check them out."

He squinted at her. "You ran their diagnostics already, right? That's what you told dispatch."

She nodded. "I had them go through it all, yes. Everything seemed fine." She noticed a spot of white on the nearest wall. A place Squeaky had painted. "But they're not." She gave a quick summary of their behavior.

Dean shot her a puzzled look. "You didn't ask them to do any of those things?"

"No. Why would I ask them to--?"

He snorted. "Dancing and singing? Never heard that before." He shook his head. "Anyway, the 'nostic checks almost everything a device would. Only thing left is close observation." He clasped his hands together then pulled them apart. "Then I'll rip them open if have to." He chuckled softly.

"Those sentries were expensive, Mr. Shuer."

He waved dismissively. "Anything I'll do will be proper, miss. Don't you worry." He motioned to the right. "Okay. I'm headed that way now."

Kate nodded. She couldn't help but feel nervous as Dean moved down the hall alone, though. Enough that she wanted to follow his every step.

Technicians tended to not like gawkers. Some even charged more if you watched.

Would it be wrong to call and make sure that he was a SenTech employee? She studied his back as he retreated, then looked at her office. Given her current circumstances, was *any* response unreasonable?

She settled on sending a quick "repairman arrived" message to the company. Given the weather conditions, that wouldn't seem too strange. It might even be considered thoughtful.

Her mind returned to the deliveryman, Ted. Did *he* think her paranoid? Was he laughing along with other deliverymen right now about that crazy Kate at the hospice? The one who thought robots were her problem?

She scowled. She really *was* paranoid now, wasn't she?

She returned to her office and her work.

9.

A loud rap on the office window broke Kate's concentration. She glanced at the time—seven o'clock! Almost two hours had passed since she'd let the repairman in. Where had the time gone?

She stood and checked the halls. She could see Lucy and Fred near the end of the leftmost hall, looking normal. Mr. Shuer was directly outside her office. He waved his device at her and then opened the door.

If nothing else, he was bold.

"Hello," she said. "What have you learned?"

He raised the device. "Got through the lot of them." He glanced at her. "All of them were behind in their system updates. A couple weeks out-of-date in fact."

She nodded. "I didn't know that. So, do I—"

"I updated them for you. Got them caught up to the latest. Should solve a lot of issues."

She leaned against her desk and smiled. "Would that fix what I've been seeing? The strange stuff?"

Dean shrugged. "I'd like to say 'yes,' but to be honest, I don't think so. What you described seems sort of random." He frowned. "I didn't observe anything like that."

Kate's heart sank. "So, you found nothing wrong?" She glanced up the hall again. Lucy and Fred were gone. Dante was moving slowly between rooms now, carrying a duster. "That can't be."

"Hey, I didn't say 'nothing.'" Dean stepped closer and showed her his handheld device. On it was a graph with five red lines. All had peaks and valleys. "I recorded some anomalies in their processing. This shows their thought-lines over the last couple days. See those little blips there?" He indicated places where the lines seemed to ripple. "That's the anomalies."

The lines meant little to her, of course, but she tried to look interested. Made more difficult by the repairman's proximity. It was nothing overly suggestive, but the side of his body was now touching hers. Unnecessarily so, she thought.

Also, Dean smelled funny. Not awful or unwashed. More like an electronic device that was shorting out. "What would cause anomalies like that?" she asked.

He looked at her. "Thought maybe you could tell me."

She shook her head. "I...I have no idea."

His eyes narrowed. "Really, Kate? Because..." He leaned away and made a swiping motion with his hand. "I mean, I don't want to make any accusations here, but—"

"Accusations?"

He shrugged. "Well, the last time I saw graphs like this, the client had been..." He placed a hand on his chin and looked at the ceiling. "How can I say this delicately? 'Tampering' is the best word I can think of."

"Tampering?"

He shrugged. "Corporate has lots of nice words to cover sentry misuse."

"Misuse...?"

Dean raised a hand. "Hey, don't take this personal." He made a show of checking the halls. "Are there other folks who have regular access to your machines?"

Kate's stomach knotted. "The guests see the sentries often."

He frowned. "Yeah, I saw your guests. I don't think they're the issue." He leaned closer. "They seem more concerned with living another day, you know?"

She bristled. "That's not the way I'd phrase it, Mr. Shuer."

"But it's true, ain't it? I mean, no offense and all but—"

She drew her arms tight across her chest. "What are you getting at?"

He indicated the now-empty halls. "Just saying that someone could get a little stir crazy out here. Especially with all the dying going on." He removed his hat and put it over his chest. "No disrespect in that, miss. It's a hard thing, watching stuff shuffle off. Had that experience more than once in my day."

She felt uncomfortable again. She straightened to be as imposing as possible. "What are you implying, Mr. Shuer?"

He scanned her office, eyes eventually finding the picture of her parents. "Ever hear of the uncanny valley, Miss Kate?"

"I've heard the term, yes, but—"

"Yeah, good." He nodded. "Today's synthetics straddle the edge of it. I mean, they're made to be like us, right? They have arms and voices and..." He opened his arms as if to hug something. "...a real presence."

He smiled. "They're not *too* human, though. Not so much that we get repulsed by them. So, it's easy for them to become companions. Like dogs or cats. To settle into that place of assumed friendship." He pointed at his device. "Especially models like your sentries. They're made to care for people, after all. To feed them and bathe them." He shrugged again. "Some folks just take the connection too far. Start taking their machines out to shows and whatnot."

Kate felt warmth in her face. "You are a disgusting little man."

He raised both hands defensively. "Hey now, don't be like that. I'm only going on what I know from experience. It's a documented thing. Sentries that are asked to—" He stopped himself, took a breath, and assumed a softer tone. "Sentries that operate outside their normal roles, that are put into situations they're not designed for, can suffer repercussions. Functional misfires. That's all I'm saying." He patted the SenTech insignia on his overalls. "They aren't made for that. Aren't warrantied for it either."

"I'm uncomfortable with this conversation." She pointed toward the door. "I think you should leave."

"You're taking offense," he said. "You shouldn't take offense. I'm only doing my job."

She stepped around him to the office door. "Please, leave," she said, motioning him out.

He moved to the hall but remained close. "We haven't solved your problem," he said. "Your sentries should be wiped and refitted. That'll get their thought lines back to normal." He pointed at her. "And all tasks beyond their designations should end, Miss Kate. As uncomfortable as that might be."

She narrowed her eyes. "Listen to me carefully, *Dean*. Our sentries are not, nor have they ever been—"

He raised his hands again. "Okay, okay, forget what I said." He smiled. "But you know, companionship for someone like yourself shouldn't be difficult."

She said nothing. Only stared.

"I mean, you're not bad looking." He straightened the front of his overalls. "Maybe a little uptight, but that's not uncommon."

She felt vulnerable and on edge, but she'd been in this kind of situation before. Confidence was a good defense. Plus, there was a distress signal she could use. Back at her desk.

She pointed at the door.

He shook his head. "Seriously, I'm trying to help. Maybe I could—" He glanced at the entry door. "Is there any place to eat around here? I'll buy you dinner."

"Go! Now!"

He slumped slightly but turned and walked toward the door. When he reached it, he raised his device. "The bill will be sent along with my diagnosis and recommendations for correction."

She crossed her arms. "I'm sorry, Mr. Shuer, but I don't agree with your diagnosis."

He patted his chest. "I'm the expert, remember? Why I'm paid the big bucks." He smiled. "I have to file a report, Kate. That's how it works."

Was he threatening her now? Was this whole thing a scam? A play for more money, or dates, or something? She glanced at her desk. "You won't do any such thing," she said. "In fact, if you attempt to label me as someone who does anything strange, I'll call your superiors and let them know what you're up to."

"Up to?" He gave her a sideways look. "Hey, lady, I'm not up to anything. You're the one that's got something..." He shook his head. "I don't know what you're up to." He pointed his device at her and scowled. "Are you threatening me?"

Something about his tone made her retreat inside. Perhaps she'd pushed too far. All she really wanted was for him to leave. "No," she said. "But there's no way of knowing your intent, is there? You could easily use this as a racket. You're the expert, right? You could say that the sentries have been misused and use that to blackmail—or worse—your unknowing clients." She gripped the side of the office doorway. It felt cool and strong.

"Eh?" Dean said. "What do you mean?"

"That's not what you're doing, correct? You're not trying to extort money from me, or force me into a night out, or anything like that, are you?" She glanced at the external windows. It was still snowing.

Dean removed his cap, scratched his head, and repositioned the cap again. "No...no...nothing like that. I was just..." He attached the device to his hip. "Tell you what, Kate, I'll comp my time here." He raised a shoulder. "All I did was download some updates, after all. Not much work in that." He grabbed the door's handle and cracked it open.

The temperature dropped dramatically. Kate instinctively drew her arms around herself. "I don't mind paying for your time," she said. "I wouldn't have known what to check."

"Nah, it's okay." He pulled the door open further. Snow filled the air around him. "Didn't let up, did it? I better get going or I won't get back. Huve or no."

He gave her a last, once-over look that ended with a forced smile. "Thank you for your patronage." He walked out and the door thumped heavily behind him.

10.

Kate fought the urge to sprint to the door and ensure it was locked. Instead, she waited ten seconds before drifting over and checking it. She checked outside through one of the side windows too. No sign of Mr. Shuer's vehicle.

She took a deep breath and let it out slowly. Good. The strange, little man was gone.

Her stomach reminded her she hadn't eaten in a while. She should make a quick walkthrough of the building and retire for the evening. Aside from the technician's visit, it had been an uneventful afternoon. No singing or dancing sentries. No comedy.

She turned and found Fred standing right behind her. She let out a clipped scream.

The sentry's arms went wide, and his head lifted. "My apologies, Director, did I startle you?"

"Yes," she said, then chuckled. "You did, a little. Yes."

Fred's head lowered. "Again, I'm sorry."

She glanced at Fred's legs. "I'm surprised I didn't hear you. I usually notice."

Fred indicated the floor. "There is carpeting here."

She noted the entry mat and the outline of a lamb it displayed. "Yes...right."

"Also, Mr. Shuer upgraded my system," Fred said. "Perhaps that helped?"

"Yes...maybe..." It was difficult to forget Dean's allegations. They were nonsense, of course, but was there a glimmer of truth there? Did she rely too heavily on artificial lives? Would the Keep be better with human caretakers? They wouldn't be as efficient, or as cheap, but still...

"There's a storm," Fred said.

"What's that?"

Fred indicated the windows. "Outside. A winter storm that includes high winds and heavy accumulation."

She nodded. Glanced at the door again. "So, I've seen." There was a dusting of snow still on the end of the mat. Made it look like the lamb was sitting in a snowbank.

"It will make any evening plans difficult," Fred said. "If you wanted to go out, I mean."

She shook her head. "No problem there," she said. "I'm going to do a last check here. Everyone okay?"

"As much as can be expected. Mrs. Daulton is comatose."

She nodded, knowing that probably wasn't a good sign. "Anything else?"

"All part of the process, Director. I suspect she won't survive the night. I've notified her close relations, but given the weather..."

Kate nodded. "Understood. Make sure she's comfortable. And all the monitoring devices are functional."

"Already done."

Kate frowned. Another room soon would be empty. Another loss of someone she hardly knew. She thought of Ted again. Would it be wrong to call him? She could use the excuse of wanting an update...even though it had only been a few hours.

She shook her head. Too desperate and lonely.

"What's wrong, Kate?" Fred said.

She touched the sentry's lower left arm. "Nothing, Fred. Let's go check things over."

Fred waved his upper right arm. "Right this way!"

An hour and a half later, Kate took her place on the couch in her apartment. Her belly was full, her apartment was warm, and her attention span waned. She heard the wind blowing outside and the occasional gust of snow scratch against the windowpane like sand. It was a good night to stay in—regardless of whether she'd planned to go out or not.

She attempted to focus on her book—the novel *Dracula* that she'd found in one of the patients' rooms—but even the story's tense plotting couldn't engage her tired mind. Little of what she'd experienced duplicated the protagonist Harker's experiences in the story. He was in the grip of clear evil. His only course was to fight or die.

She didn't know what she was experiencing at all. In fact, if Mr. Shuer was to be believed, the sentries' misbehavior was of her own making! She'd somehow pushed them beyond their normal roles and caused them to malfunction.

She chuckled at the absurdity. She was safe and warm inside while a storm raged outside. That was the reality of her life. She was a center of competence amid an otherwise stormy world.

The room's lights dimmed. It was a little presumptuous on the AI's part—she wasn't asleep yet—but she didn't ask that they be turned up again. She only snuggled deeper into her blanket and listened to the storm rage. The scratching sound on the window. Everything was good. Fine. She had a warm place and a rewarding, useful job. She had up-to-date sentries and her whole life ahead of her.

The wind's howl took on a more rhythmic tone, becoming more like the ebb and flow of a surf. Surge and then still. Rise and fall.

"Here we go again," she said, barely conscious. "More oceans and stars."

The room darkened excepting the pinprick of stars. She soon found herself floating above the couch, spacesuit, and helmet again in place.

"How is this happening?"

She waved her arms and gasped, looking toward the floor. "Can I roll?" She tucked her head and tried. It was a slow process, but she finally completed a 360 degree turn while remaining above the ground.

"That was amazing." She looked toward the starfield. "I was never good at tumbling." She pointed toward the side of her head. "Inner ear strangeness. I usually got dizzy and threw up."

"You've missed a lot." The warm and distant voice.

She shook her head. "I don't think so. I think I've been busy. Accomplished a lot."

"The joy of work."

"Yes."

"Also, a curse. Cursed is the ground because of you."

She smiled and pointed down. "The ground is a long way away now."

"Is it?" The voice seemed to fade as did the stars. Kate heard a chirp from the AI and felt herself falling. A second later, she found that she was back on the couch. The storm still raged. Loud and forceful.

The chirp repeated. That part hadn't been a dream. "What is it?" she groaned out.

"There's someone at the front door," the AI said.

Kate checked the time. Almost nine o'clock. Late, but not too late. Who could it be? Possibly one of Mrs. Daulton's relatives come to say goodbye. She called for the lights and stood. She glanced down at herself. She'd changed to more relaxing clothes since work—casual pants and a sweatshirt—but she was still presentable. Not too wrinkled or stained.

She found her shoes and made her way out of the apartment, down a short flight of stairs, and around a corner to the door to the Keep proper. It was an older, painted-wood model that required a heavy tug to open. Through it, she emerged into the northmost main hall.

The Keep's lights were dim and the facility quiet except for a few distant clicks and beeps. She heard a thump on the front door then and hurried toward it. The guests were all in some way sedated, sure, but loud thumps were never welcome.

She reached the entryway foyer and froze. Though the snow was fog-like outside, she could clearly see the silhouette of a large vehicle parked there. At first, she thought it was another delivery truck, but then a break in the snow revealed a familiar design on the vehicle's side: SenTech.

Dean Shuer had returned.

11.

Ice ran down Kate's spine. This, in addition to the cold Kate felt emanating through the door and windows, caused her to pull her sweatshirt closer to her body.

Why was he back?

As she contemplated what to do, Dean leaned over to one of the side windows and pressed his hand-shielded face against it. He noticed her and waved. "Hey! I need help! Open the door!"

She hesitated, glancing back at the office and the location of the alarm. She also contemplated calling one of the sentries. It would be company if nothing else.

Was she overreacting? Maybe he—

Dean knocked on the door again.

She checked the window, noting a dark smear his hand had left behind. Was that blood? Was he injured?

Still groggy, she moved forward and unlocked the door. It was all she could do to get out of the way as Dean's weight swung it open.

His eyes met hers briefly, then he coughed and fell forward onto the mat. He remained there—wheezing and propped on one hand—as if trying to recover from a long race. His breath formed clouds in the air. Clouds that grew and moved and mingled with her own.

"Are you—?"

He coughed again. "Freezing," he said. "Near dying."

Noting the storm's howl, she stepped around him and shut the door. Gingerly, she placed a hand on his back, still covered by a too-thin coat. "What can I do, Mr. Shuer?"

He coughed and groaned. "Been a devil of a night, Miss Kate."

He started to rise, so she instinctively threw an arm around him and helped him up. She detected the sour shorted-wire smell again, though it was muted, frozen by the cold. When Dean was fully standing, she slid around in front of him. She saw blood on his left hand, running down his fingers from a wound near his palm. "You're cut!"

She hurried around the corner to a nearby linen closet. Along the way, she noticed Lucy in the hall and motioned for her. Kate then grabbed a small towel and returned to the foyer. Dean moved beyond the foyer now to the inner doors. There were circles of blood down the length of the entry mat.

Dean noticed her gaze. "I made a mess here, sorry. I'll clean it up."

She gave him the towel which he immediately wrapped around his hand. "A sentry can clean it later," she said. "What happened?"

"Slid off the road, believe it or not."

"In your hover?"

He nodded once. "Hard to believe, I know. But the wind—" He motioned toward the front door. "And the drifts. Lots of them. Big ones." He raised a shoulder. "Anyway, I went off. Got out to push and near froze to death. Managed to get it back on a flat surface." He raised his injured hand. "One of the mirrors caught a tree. Cut myself." He looked at the mat where blood now dotted the lamb's face. "Stupid, I know. Lots of stupid."

"Not stupid," she said. "Just the sort of thing that happens."

He smiled halfheartedly. "Nice of you to say."

Lucy reached them. "How can I help you, Director?"

"Mr. Shuer has an injured right hand," Kate said. "Can you dress it, please?"

"Yes, of course." Lucy raised a lower arm and moved toward the repairman.

Dean watched the sentry as it approached. "Eh, are you sure this—?"

"Is within the sentry's normal operating procedures?" Kate said. "Yes, I'm sure it is."

Dean frowned but hesitantly raised his towel-wrapped appendage.

Lucy gripped the arm with one hand and removed the towel with another. "This is a deep cut. How did it happen?"

Dean winced as Lucy drew the hand close. "Why do you want to know?" he said.

"He cut it on a mirror," Kate said.

Lucy looked Kate's way and lowered her head a few centimeters. "Curious. I would've expected a metal object."

"It might have been metal," Dean said. "I mean, the casing is metal. So yeah, probably metal."

Lucy studied the hand again. "The wound should be sutured. Do I have your permission to do so?"

"Is it going to hurt?"

"Doctor, it hurts when I do this," Lucy muttered. "Then don't do that!" She made a low, chuckling sound.

"What's that?" Dean asked.

"I'm sorry," Lucy said. "The suture won't hurt more than the pain you are currently experiencing. Shall I proceed?"

Kate wondered if Dean had noticed the sentry's joke but decided not to ask. "You'll numb it, of course," Kate said.

"Of course," Lucy said.

Dean gave her a worried look. "I guess that's okay then. Go ahead."

"Very good." Lucy's hands worked in concert, holding Dean's hand still, numbing it, then stitching and bandaging it. The whole procedure was over in minutes.

Lucy released Dean's hand and moved away. "How is it now, Mr. Shuer?"

Dean checked both sides of his hand, then flexed it gingerly. "Fine," he said. "Feels fine."

"I'm pleased." Lucy looked at Kate. "Do you require my presence any longer?"

Kate frowned slightly. "Is there somewhere you need to be?"

"Not for fifteen minutes," Lucy said.

"Then please stay close for a bit."

Lucy bobbed her head. "I will do so." She moved to a spot near the front of Kate's office and waited.

Dean looked at himself, then brushed at the front of his coat and pants. "Really made myself a mess here, huh? All this blood and dirt." He looked at her. "I must look a wreck."

"You're fine," Kate said, unsure of what else to say. In truth, aside from a few bloodstains, Dean didn't look that different than when she'd first met him. The real question was: What now? She checked the front windows. The storm continued.

Dean glanced at the windows too. "Anyway..." He lifted his hand. "I rarely get to see the machines work like that."

"They're quite effective." Kate suddenly felt conspicuous in her casual clothes. Less able to project the confidence she'd projected before. It was almost like Dean was inside her apartment.

Dean chuckled. "They're really something, those machines." He scratched under his cap. "Listen, I'm not sure what to do here. I don't think I can drive like this. And those winds—"

"Is there someone I could call?" She asked. "Someone who might pick you up?"

He shook his head. "Nobody like that, no. I'm by myself unless you count my hamster." He smiled at her. "Do you like pets?"

"I can't offer you a bed here," Kate blurted out. "Sorry. There are regulations. If I use rooms outside their intended purpose—"

He balled his hands. Scowled. "You're using that on me now? Because I said that to you about your machines?"

She took a half step back. Toward the office. Toward Lucy. "Wasn't picking a fight, Mr. Shuer. I just have rules to follow. Government rules."

He stared at her a moment, then shook his head and thumped his chest as if chastising himself. "Oh right, sure. Sorry." He held up a hand. "Of course, you'd have things like that. I have things like that. Nuisance government things." He motioned toward the foyer. "Maybe I could just camp out on the floor here until morning?" He looked at the mat. "Probably won't be too bad. I'll just try to avoid the blood." He pointed a thumb at the windows. "Might be a little cold. Could I maybe borrow a blanket or two?"

She didn't want Dean in the building. It not only broke protocol, but it also wasn't safe for the patients. A strange person wandering around vulnerable people all night? Even if they were only a few guests, it seemed wrong.

It was an unusual situation, though. The storm. Dean's accident and injury. The hour.

"I understand," Dean said. "Understand you don't like me." He shrugged. "I said things..." He put out his hands, palms up. "It was an uncomfortable topic, okay?" He smiled. "No one likes the messenger, right?" He shook his head. "I don't know about sleeping in the truck, though. I don't have enough fuel to keep it going all night, and it's really cold."

"There's a lodge about five miles back," Kate offered.

Dean glanced up the hall to his right. "Five miles, you say? Didn't see any hotels that way."

"There's one there. Called 'Candy Cove.' They have a sign by the road."

"'Candy Cove?'" He snorted. "Sounds like a kids' place." Another head shake. "Anyway, I'm sure I missed it. You can't see nothing out there."

Kate glanced up the hallway to her right, eyes lighting on the door that led to her apartment. Only a few minutes ago, she'd been there, enjoying a nap. Feeling safe from the storm. Protected. She closed her hands together as if praying. "Listen, I would like to help you, but you can't stay here. It isn't that sort of facility."

Dean grunted and furrowed his brow. "Where do *you* stay?" He pointed his injured hand at her. "You don't seem dressed for work there."

She pulled her arms around herself. "That's none of your business."

"Hey, I—"

"You've made me uncomfortable again, Mr. Shuer. Please leave now."

Dean's face flushed with color. "But the storm! My hand!"

"We've bandaged your hand. Now go."

Dean squared his stance. "You can't do that. It isn't right."

"This is my facility. I have every right. I will call the police if—"

He laughed. "How are they going to get here?"

"They have vehicles that fly."

"That they'll bring out here in this? You're crazy, Miss."

She did her best to seem resilient. Strong. "You should go while you still can. Five miles is not far."

Dean stomped a foot onto the lamb's face. "I'm staying here, whether you like it or not."

12.

Her discomfort reached a new level. "I've been polite," Kate said. "I won't ask again."

Dean reached into his toolbelt, but instead of his screened device, he brought out a long, silver-bladed object. "Didn't want to do this," he said. "You being so friendly and all. Fixing my hand and letting me out of the weather, but..." He shook his head. "Seems you can't understand logic."

Kate turned and ran for the office and the com. Before she reached the door, Lucy stepped in front of her. "Do you require anything, Director?"

Kate placed a hand on Lucy's left shoulder and pushed. The sentry didn't budge.

Lucy's head extended so her eyes were level with Kate's. "Director?"

"What are you doing?" Kate removed her hand from Lucy and attempted to squeeze around the sentry. "I need you to get out of the way."

"I'm unable to do that, Kate."

Dean laughed.

She gave the sentry another desperate shove. "What are you talking about? Just move!"

But Lucy didn't move. She raised her arms instead, further blocking the office door. "Can I help you, Director?"

Kate looked at Dean, who thankfully, hadn't moved from the welcome mat. "Why won't Lucy move?"

Dean gave her a smug look, then brought out his screened device. "Because I didn't want it to," he said. "I updated its system, remember?"

Kate's hands felt numb. Her heart pounded in her chest. "What did you do?"

Dean stepped closer. "A few minor adjustments. I needed to be sure they wouldn't bother me when I came back."

"So, you were planning this earlier today?"

"Months ago, actually."

"Months ago?"

Dean moved close enough that Kate could detect the shorted wire smell. "When I was here for your last maintenance? You don't remember?"

She remembered a string of service calls, but none that concerned the sentries specifically. That didn't mean the update didn't happen. There was always something that required her attention.

Would she forget Dean, though? She didn't think so.

He wasn't the man who'd stared at her, was he?

She studied his face. He might be.

Dean snorted. "I can see your wheels spinning. You wouldn't remember me anyway, would you? I know your type."

"I really don't think you were here," she said. "Why would I have called you?"

He shrugged. "Doesn't matter." He waved the device. "All that matters now is that your sentries obey me."

Kate gasped and bolted for the rightmost hallway. If she could make it to the end, she could reach her apartment. From there, she could escape—

Well, no, she couldn't, because of the storm. But she could at least lock herself in and get a message out to the authorities. That would be enough.

She made it past Suite A, one of the empties, and was nearing B when she heard Dean chuckle behind her. She glanced back and saw him still standing near the entranceway.

What was he laughing about?

Dante appeared from Suite B to her right, and with all four arms open, lunged at her. She avoided its embrace but collided with the wall near where Squeaky had painted.

This scene was darker, though. It showed people running and screaming below an unknown terror from the sky. It caused her to stall long enough for Dante to grab her shirt sleeve. She yelped, pulled away, but didn't get free.

Dante's left arms reached for her. She jerked again and her sleeve ripped. She ran for the hall exit, tearing the sleeve more as she went.

Dean laughed again.

The sleeve pulled off completely, freeing her. She sprinted ahead.

How ridiculous was this? Pursued by her own sentries! And with a maniacal repairman in charge. It was like something from that Dracula novel, except she had no idea how to make it stop. No crucifix, garlic, or stake. She didn't even have a friend to call on. Only invalids and machines.

She focused on the door. On her escape. That's all she could hope for. Reaching her place and barricading herself in.

"Why do they always run?" Dean said. "No time for the tech guy."

She could hear multiple sentries click-click-clicking their way behind her. Who else was back there now, besides Dante? Lucy? Fred? It didn't matter. All that mattered was the door. She slid the last meter to it, gripped the handle, and pulled.

It resisted her efforts. Stupid old door. Why hadn't she had it fixed? Or at least oiled it? She planted her feet and gave it another pull. It burst open this time, causing her to fall—sprawling—on the floor.

And beyond it, was Squeaky.

Squeaky raised all four arms as if to embrace her. "Can I help you, Director?"

Still seated on the floor, Kate crab-walked to the wall and then up it to stand. Though she never thought of the sentries as particularly fast on their feet, she wasn't sure she could easily dodge Squeaky's arms. Those appendages were exceedingly fast, and in the case of the lower arms, might also be pointy and sharp.

She looked back the way she'd come. Two more of the sentries—Lucy and Sally—had joined Dante near Suite B. All three had the same arms-wide embracing pose as Squeaky. It was eerie and frightening.

Dean stood just outside of Suite A. When he saw her looking, he pointed at the room. "This one is free. I could've slept here." He brought a hand to his chin. "Maybe I will sleep here..." He shook his head then and strolled her way. "First, I want to see where you sleep, though. I bet it's lots better."

Kate waited, uncertain what to do next. Slowly, Squeaky moved up from behind, squeaking with every step. In front, Dante and the others moved steadily closer. Could she avoid them all and reach the front door? Doubtful.

And even if she did get outside, what then? Run off into a blizzard? Steal Dean's hover? What?

She fought the instinct to cry, focusing instead on her reoccurring dreams. Those filled with oceans and stars.

Squeaky gripped her shoulder. It was a gentle touch, but like the hand itself, hid a metal firmness underneath. One that could be applied in an instant.

Crossing her arms, she waited for the others to reach her. The sentries stopped about a meter away, but Dean came to within centimeters. Smiled. "You won't forget me now, will you?"

"What are you doing?" she said. "Kidnapping me?"

He pointed his knife at her. "You said you'd report me to work. I can't let you do that."

"I won't," she said. "I haven't. So, let's simply part ways."

"But there's the storm..." He looked toward the entryway, then smiled again. "We can make the best of a bad situation."

She tightened her arms to suppress a shiver. "I don't see how."

"I need a place to stay. And you need company. *Human* company."

"You wouldn't be my first choice."

He laughed and made a show of looking all around. "Well, I don't see many options."

"Even if you were the only option," she said, "the answer would be 'no.'"

He snorted. "You're a sad case."

It was Kate's turn to laugh. "I'm not the one threatening a caregiver."

He made a grunting noise and lunged toward her before pulling up short. She instinctively cowered backwards, bumping into Squeaky's torso. The sentry's hand tightened on her shoulder and another hand grabbed her left elbow.

"You're infuriating!" Dean said.

"Another reason we should part ways."

Dean thought for a moment, then raised a finger. "You're right. Relationships are too complicated." He waved the knife at her. "It's time to end this one."

"So, you're going to kill me now?" She did her best to maintain a confident exterior while wondering how difficult it would be to break free of Squeaky. She might have to rip her shirt more, but the shirt was already a loss. The least of her worries. The door to her apartment. If only she could reach it.

Dean placed his knife in Sally's uppermost right hand. "No, *I'm* not going to kill you. Your sentry here will."

She shook her head. "Sentries can't kill. They're made to preserve life as long as possible."

"You expect me to believe that?" Dean waved his hands in the air. "This place is where people come to die. Sentries let that happen. That's part of their programming."

He was correct there. It was a specialized distinction of the sentry design—to let nature take its course. To avoid life-saving measures when asked to. "They can't hurt, though," she said. "Not like that."

He waved his device. "Part of the testing protocol. I'll just make it think you're a cadaver. Then it will be free to operate." Another smile. "Can't hurt something that's already dead, right?"

She jerked against Squeaky and managed to free her shoulder. His grip on her left elbow remained, though. She tugged until it hurt but couldn't get loose. She grunted and swore.

"You'll injure yourself," Squeaky said. "Let me help you, Director." He caught her beneath the shoulders and lifted her away from the floor.

She kicked and tried to reach for the ground. "Put me down," she said. "As your Director, I order you to let me go." She pointed at Dean. "Restrain him!"

Dean shook his head. "Pitiful." He searched the area around them. "Now, where to do our surgery? Where would make the most sense?" He stepped to the left and looked past Squeaky. "This time of night, the best place would probably be where you're most likely to be."

He pointed to the hallway door behind them. "Let's go to her place."

13.

Five minutes later, they were in Kate's apartment. Dean remained near the entry door, while Squeaky carried Kate to the couch with Lucy tagging along. The rest of the sentries stayed in the hospice after Dean cleared their memories of everything Dean-related. They were now going about their duties. Monitoring the remaining patients and maintaining Lamb's Keep.

Dean brought a hand to his chin and his eyes darted between the living area and the adjoining kitchen. "Probably best to do this in here," he said, indicating the living room. "On the couch would make it look more like a suicide." He shrugged. "Of course, in the kitchen...well, there's lots of ways to cut yourself there. Might be an accidental death. You just couldn't reach anyone because of the storm."

Kate didn't try to wrestle free as Squeaky placed her in a seated position. She wouldn't have been able to go anywhere anyway. The sentry's lower hands never left her shoulders.

"Why?" she mumbled. "Why do want to—?"

"Because you threatened my job?" he said. "Because you wouldn't let me stay here? Either is reason enough." He addressed the sentries. "What do you think?"

"You'll doubtless be caught," Lucy said.

Squeaky raised his head. "Cameras, electronic traces, synthetic memories. All could be used."

Kate attempted to straighten despite Squeaky's hands. "That's right. They'll find you."

Dean laughed loudly. "I don't think so. This isn't the first...extra service I've provided to a customer."

So, like Dracula, he had a history of predatory behavior. "You've been shedding DNA since you arrived," she said. "You can't cover all that."

"I have faith in your sentries' ability to clean up. I hear they're quite efficient." He snapped his fingers and ducked into the kitchen. He returned with a long-bladed knife. "Wouldn't be a good idea to waste my own knife now, would it?" He swapped the knife with the one Lucy held. "Yours seems sharper than mine, anyway. Quicker."

"AI, call the police," Kate said.

"Calling," the AI said.

Dean looked panicked for a moment. "Stop calling," he said. "Master code 5211 and erase."

"Understood," the AI said.

Dean shook his finger at her. "That was a good move there. I should've anticipated that one." He smiled. "Good thing I trained in house AIs." He removed his cap to tap his head. "Master codes are still up here."

"Were you the reason the sentries malfunctioned?" she asked.

Dean shrugged and looked worriedly around the room again. "You'll never know, will you?"

Kate searched the room too, hoping to find something, anything, that could help her. But there were only her creature comforts—warm chairs, wooden floor, and the entertainment cabinet. "Did you make the stuff happen here too, somehow?" she asked, noticing the console's lights.

"What stuff?" he said.

"The dreams," she said. "The visions of space. The floating sea animals?"

Dean squinted at her. "Space and sea animals?"

She pointed at the ceiling and the walls. "Right. They seemed to float right there. Like holograms, but they were so real. Like I could touch them. Feel them."

"Wow..." Dean said. "I thought I had issues." He brought out his device, checked something on the screen, and pointed at Lucy. "How do you perceive the body on the couch, sentry?"

Lucy looked Kate's direction. "I see a donor for an emergency heart transplant." She lifted the arm holding the knife. "An operation is required."

Kate gasped and struggled against Squeaky's grip.

Lucy moved closer and addressed Squeaky directly. "Put the patient in a prone position."

Kate continued to fight but accomplished nothing. Squeaky restrained her arms with his right hands and used the other two to first grasp her torso, then lift her and place her on her back.

Lucy restrained Kate's feet, then Dean came over and reached out a hand. "Let me help with those. You might need all four hands for the work."

Kate screamed and attempted to kick. Dean held tightly, though, and smiled. "See there, I already have a task for your extra arms," he said to Lucy. "Please use one to cover the patient's mouth." He winked and his smile broadened. "Wouldn't want to wake the invalids, would we?"

Kate was tempted to bite Lucy's hand as it pressed against her face. It wouldn't help, of course. Sentries didn't feel pain. They only tried to stop it. And in this case, Lucy thought she was helping, even as she was silencing Kate.

How ironic. Dying at the hands of something intended to help. Murdered by emotionless metal and plastic machines.

Dean's face was the picture of evil, grinning subtly as he clung to her feet. After all the years of distancing herself, of walling herself off emotionally, Kate would die with an example of raw and unbalanced humanity holding her down. More irony.

She thought of Ted. If she'd been a little more accessible, maybe he'd be calling her now. Or they might even be out on a date. Stuck somewhere cozy and bright until the storm settled. What would happen when he called with information about Mr. Flit? Would he be shocked to hear that she was dead? Would he ever even know?

"Are you ready to begin?" Dean asked.

Lucy's head bobbed up and down. "I will expose the chest now." Lucy's knife-wielding hand deftly cut a new opening in the front of Kate's shirt.

Kate felt coolness on her upper chest. She became aware of Dean's gaze. It was an awful thing. Like a snake slithering from the couch onto her body. Though still mostly covered, she felt exposed and fragile. She shut her eyes and tried to descend into the cushions.

She thought about the Lamb's Keep patients. Would they be okay without her? Would the sentries maintain them until someone else arrived? And who would find her body? Another delivery person? Relatives come to give their final regards?

This couldn't be happening. She squirmed and fought. How was this happening?

"I'm preparing to open the chest cavity," Lucy said. "Applying local anesthesia now."

"That's not necessary," Dean said. "The patient is already sedated."

"Ah, very good," Lucy said. "I will open now."

Dean's grip tightened around her feet. Squeaky's grip remained steadfast. Clinical and cool. Kate pried open her eyes long enough to see Lucy's knife hand—the lower right one—slowly descending.

How odd that it was slow. Sentries rarely did anything slow.

This was heart surgery though, wasn't it? It needed to be precise. Calculated. Deliberate.

Closer and closer the hand came. Kate attempted to scream again, but no sound got through Lucy's hand. Kate couldn't even move now for all the hands upon her. She couldn't scream or shudder.

My heart will explode, she thought. Explode and save Dean the trouble.

The blade touched her skin.

And the room went dark.

14.

Dean swore and yelled at the AI. "Turn the lights back on!"

No response. No change to the lighting either.

Dean swore again. "Did you forget to pay your power bill?" he asked.

Kate could only squirm in response. Dean seemed to realize this then because he asked for Lucy to uncover her mouth.

Kate tried to take a deep breath then felt the blade, still poised on her chest. The room's ambient light was barely enough to see the shadows that held her.

"You heard me," Dean said. "Why are the lights off?"

"Maybe it's the storm," she whispered.

He grunted and looked toward the windows. "Yeah, I guess that's possible."

Dean's grip eased on Kate's ankles. She contemplated attempting to kick free, but the knife's presence stopped her. "Can you put away the knife for a second?" she asked.

His focus remained on the windows and door. "Yeah, um...no, I'm trying to figure out what to do here."

Kate heard only the wind as Dean thought. Again, she contemplated kicking. Again, the nearness of the knife gave her pause.

Dean grunted. "No, wait," He looked at Lucy. "You sentries don't need lights to operate, do you?"

"I'm able to self-illuminate," Lucy said. "Would you like me to do so?"

"Of course. Right away."

A light turned on in Lucy's chest, producing a circle of illumination over Kate's midsection.

"That's better," Dean said. "Why don't you do that too there, other sentry?"

Squeaky turned its light on, blinding Kate in the process.

"Okay. We're back in business." Dean smiled. "Let's get this—"

Kicking a foot free, Kate brought her heel down hard on Dean's hands. He yelped and swore. He spent the next thirty seconds trying to reclaim control of her loose appendage while she did her best to keep that from happening. Dean eventually won, primarily because of the still-too-close knife.

"All. Right. Now." Dean seethed. "No more delays. Sentry—"

There was a knock on the door. He growled softly, then handed Kate's feet to Lucy.

In the process, the knife lifted from Kate's chest. She took a deep breath and let it out slowly. Someone was at the door! If only she could—

"Were you expecting someone?" Dean asked.

Lucy's hand remained clamped over Kate's mouth. She could only wiggle her head in response.

Dean snorted and brought out his knife again. "This is becoming way too complicated." He smiled. "Must be one of the invalids, right? Can they go wandering around at night?"

She shrugged. What else could she do?

Dean scowled. "I'm beginning to wonder about your management skills." He made a show of hiding the knife behind his back and disappeared into the gloom. A few seconds later, he asked for the visitor's name. There was no response, so Dean asked again.

Another knock followed by the sound of the door opening.

"Why are you here?" Dean asked.

"I've fulfilled all my duties," the sentry—Fred, she thought—said.

"Fulfilled all your duties? I thought you machines stayed busy all night. Cleaning and maintaining, right?" There were a couple footfalls then Dean spoke from somewhere closer. "Free her mouth for a minute."

Kate felt Lucy's grip ease and breathed deeply. She could talk again, but what to do with that freedom? There was no one around who could help.

Dean's face appeared in the glow of the sentries' lamps. "You know what your sentry is talking about?" he asked.

"It said it's done for the night," Kate said. "Seems obvious."

He nodded toward the door. "Does it always do that, though? Come here and tell you that?"

She shrugged. "What does it matter?"

Dean scowled as he thought. A few seconds later, he clapped his hands together. "Now I get it. This is part of it, isn't it?" He reentered the gloom. "Part of you using sentries beyond their abilities."

"What?" she said. "That's ridi—"

"Yeah, I bet that's it! This one is sort of a surrogate father or something. Comes to check on you at night."

"You're crazy," she said.

"I'm not any crazier than you are, sister." He laughed. "No, not at all."

"Would you like to hear a joke?" Lucy asked.

Dean quieted. "What's that?"

The storm's wail increased in volume, then decreased. Increased and decreased. Kate looked toward the windows. Oddly, she could see light outside. A cloud stretching from one end to the other. No, not a cloud. A nebula! A long band of stars.

"Would you like to know why I'm here, Director?" Fred's voice, somewhere near the door.

"Fred?" she said. "I need you to—"

"Shut her up again," Dean said. "Don't need her confusing anyone."

Lucy's hand reached for Kate's mouth. Kate struggled, turning her head back and forth. Twisting and squirming.

"I'll tell you why I'm here, Director," Fred said. There was the sound of quick footsteps, as if Fred was doing a two-step. "I'm here to dance."

15.

Next came more dancing. Fred performed a whole routine—click, click, tappity, tap, slide, tap, click. It was complicated enough that Kate wished she could see it. It was no doubt worthy of Fred's namesake.

"What is that?" Dean asked. "What in the world is that?"

"Sounds like dancing." Kate twisted toward the entrance, but Squeaky's torso blocked her view. "I wish I could watch."

"Looks like dancing to me too," Dean said. "But wow, is that way beyond its specs. You really messed these things up, lady."

More dancing. Tappity, tappity, tap. Click, click, click, slide.

"Okay, enough," Dean said. "We have work to do."

The dance's cadence—its complexity—increased.

"Seriously, I mean stop!"

Fred's movements continued, sounding like a champion dancer was in her hall.

"All right. I'm shutting you down," Dean said. "It might harm you, but it has to be done."

With a little more squirming, Kate managed to see Dean's silhouette near the door. He brought the handheld tool to his face and manipulated its screen.

Fred's dancing continued unabated. Then a few seconds later, Fred spun and deftly knocked the tool from Dean's grip.

Dean screeched and bent over to find his lost device. "Be nice if there were some lights," he murmured. "Blasted machine. Now where—"

Fred kicked the technician's posterior, sending Dean sprawling. The room lights flickered, before falling dark again. Stars appeared on the ceiling, along with the sound of the ocean.

"What the—!"

Dean's hands found his device again and he feverishly worked it.

Fred's movements became less like dance steps and more like punches and kicks. Dean barely avoided the sentry's limbs, weaving and dodging.

The synthetic landed another kick to Dean's side, and with a heavy thump, Dean careened into the kitchen counter. He caught himself and brought up his knife. Fred slapped the weapon away with his top right arm, then landed an uppercut to Dean's face with its lower left.

Dean grunted, fell to the floor, and swore. "You two!" he said, addressing Lucy and Squeaky. "This thing is malfunctioning!" He ducked one of Fred's arms. "Stop it. It's hurting me."

Fred landed a few blows in succession. Dean yelled.

Releasing Kate, the sentries moved toward the skirmish. Kate rolled off the couch, and crouching down, tried to compose herself. It was all confusion now—, the storm raging, Dean yelling, Fred dancing and kicking, stars glowing in a darkened room, and the other two sentries moving in.

Soon there were sparks and shrieks as the sentries encountered each other. Oddly, all Kate could think about was how much it would cost to repair them. They'd be lucky not to break a limb or dislocate their heads. Was that sort of damage even worth repairing? And who would she call? Not Dean, and probably not the company he worked for either.

With arms wide, Squeaky moved on Fred. Fred feigned left and dodged right. He avoided Squeaky's embrace and slapped the sentry's arms away. Lucy grabbed Fred's leftmost arms, but Fred spun and hurled Lucy up the hall.

Dean tried to escape the dueling sentries but was forced to stop when Fred charged him.

Squeaky stopped the charge. Appendages entangled.

Dean broke into the hall. He stopped a few paces away, manipulated his monitoring device, and watched the sentries.

Their behavior didn't change. It was like watching a three-way boxing match. A blur of limbs both striking and blocking. Medical-grade limbs, made to care for people, now dented and scraped.

Kate's only route of escape was blocked, and even if she were to get free, she wouldn't know where to go. Not outside. Not anywhere near Dean.

She looked at the stars, still projected on the walls. What was causing that? If not Dean, then it had to be someone on Fred's side. Someone who could help. "Not sure what your plan is," she said. "But I'm a little stuck here."

Dean looked up the hallway toward the Keep proper and his eyes widened. "What are *you* doing here?" There was a response from someone—another sentry, Kate guessed—and Dean shook his head. "We don't need any of that here, no. No sculpting allowed."

Sculpting? Who was sculpting?

A large ball of something whizzed by Dean's head. He shrieked, then turned and bolted in the opposite direction. A few seconds later, she heard the exterior door chirp and more wind.

That front door was self-locking, Kate remembered. There was no way for Dean to come back in unless he'd unlocked it. Had he?

"Knock it off, everyone!" she yelled.

The apartment lights returned, and with them, the sentries' motion ceased. A few seconds later, Squeaky, Lucy, and Fred pivoted to look her way.

"Do you need assistance, Director?" Fred said.

She shook her head, then wound past them into the hall. She passed Dante—doubtless the ball flinger—a few steps before the interior door and went around it into the Keep proper. She ran to the front door, and after making sure it was locked, slid down it to sit on the floor.

Face in hands, she wept.

Kate reported Dean to the police, but nothing could be done due to the wind and snow. So, she did a final check of the place, especially the doors, and returned to her apartment. After some water and pain medicine, she locked herself in her room. Following a few false starts, she slept soundly.

The storm raged through the night.

The next morning was sunny and calm. Dean's vehicle was discovered off the side of the road by a neighbor later in the day. It was deactivated and cold. Dean was found, frozen to death, inside. After the roads were cleared, he and his vehicle were taken away.

SenTech refunded all that Dean had charged, and after numerous apologies, offered her free sentry service for the year.

She declined.

16.

Three days later, life was as normal as it could be. Two new patient guests moved in, and the sentries handled everything as they always had. There were no misbehaviors. No singing or dancing. She'd suspected that somehow those things had been Dean's doing. Perhaps unintentionally. Perhaps by assuming control of the sentries he had broken them. He'd indicated that their systems were fragile, after all.

And the projections in her apartment? Perhaps the AI had been affected by Dean's meddling, as well. Who knew?

All she wanted now was to return to business. Keep the ship moving ahead. Immerse herself in work to hide from all that happened. All the strangeness.

Following another facility walkthrough, she returned to her office to hear her system chime. She hurried around to her desk and checked the caller. A live request from Ted.

She smiled and accepted.

Ted wore a green shirt this time, but his hair seemed as wavy as the last time they'd talked. His face was serious, though.

"I just heard what happened," he said. "I'm..." He shook his head. "Are you all right?"

"I'm fine." Through her office windows she noted Fred moving up the hall away from her. "It was weird there for a while. A little scary."

"So, this guy was a sort of tech serial killer, or something?"

She shook her head. "Still undetermined. There have been a few strange tech-related deaths lately, though." She remembered the knife poised over her chest and suppressed a shudder. "They're looking into it."

Ted nodded, looking concerned. "I know this isn't the right time, but...I'd still like to take you out." He raised a hand. "No pressure, of course, but if..." He shrugged. "If you need someone to talk to."

She pressed a finger to her lips, assuming a thoughtful pose.

"We'll go somewhere nice," he said. "Somewhere out and about."

She smiled. "Somewhere out sounds great."

He exhaled noticeably, then smiled. "Okay, good. I wasn't sure. Didn't want to rush you."

Her eyes alighted on her family photo. "I don't think it's rushing at all. I...I think I might need to be rushed."

"Really? Great! So, Friday?"

She checked the hallways again. Lucy was now sweeping the rightmost hall. "Sure. I think things will be okay here. I'm getting more help."

"More sentries?"

"No. Human help this time." She smiled. "Now, what will we talk about on our date? I want to be prepared."

Ted snapped his fingers. "That reminds me! Your patient? The guy in the chute?"

"Mr. Flit?" She'd almost forgotten.

"Yeah, that guy." He furrowed his brow.

"What?"

"Well, maybe I should save this." He smiled. "So we have something to talk about."

She leaned closer and squinted. "Don't you dare."

Ted chuckled, then swiped at his bangs. "Okay. Turns out he's a hero."

"A hero?"

"Yeah, from the time before. When the world was controlled?"

She nodded. "My folks rarely talked about it. I know there was one leader who somehow got everyone to follow him."

Ted tapped his temple. "They had devices in their brain. Connected them to everything, but also kept them in check. Controlled their thoughts."

Just like Dean had controlled her sentries. A shiver traveled down Kate's spine. She rubbed at her neck to try to erase it. "Does he have something in his head too?"

"Most of that generation does," Ted said. "There was removal surgery, but I think it was risky. Dangerous." He pushed at his bangs again. "Didn't your parents have them?"

She shook her head. "They were too young. And their parents lived outside the cities."

"Sounds like a good story," Ted said. "You'll have to tell me about it."

She smiled. "I will. Maybe at dinner?"

"Sure!"

"But Mr. Flit?"

Ted looked up as if thinking. "He seems to have had an incredible life. But he was right there when the changeover happened. He was involved and somehow freed—" He smiled. "Well, a lot happened. I think he even went into space. Or knew someone who did."

Kate looked in the direction of Flit's room. "Space, huh? Did he like the sea too?"

"You mean the ocean?" Ted's brow furrowed. "Don't know. Didn't see anything about that. Though he might've lived near the ocean once."

She nodded. "That's right. I think he did." She glanced up the hall again. Fred was paused near Mr. Flit's room, looking her direction. "I should go." She smiled. "I'll see you Friday, Ted. Say six o'clock?"

"Perfect," he said. "Look forward to it."

The connection closed and she swiped it away. She sat at her desk thinking for a few moments. Then watched as the sentries went about their rounds. She checked on Fred again and found he'd gone.

She frowned. Stood.

Fred was in Mr. Flit's room when she arrived. The blinds were partially open and sunlight streamed in, seeming twice as bright now for the snow outside. The view was a wonderland of covered trees and bushes beneath a clear, blue sky.

She squinted. "Little bright, don't you think?"

"My apologies, Director." Fred moved toward the window controls. "I will adjust—"

She waved Fred off. "Don't bother. It's pretty, even if it's bright."

The sentry bobbed his head. "Very well."

She approached the chute. "How is he today?"

The sentry drew closer to the chute too. "As good as can be expected. His chute is performing to standards, but..." He uncharacteristically laid a hand on the chute's surface. "I don't think it will be of use long."

Kate used the chute's controls to make the surface transparent. Flit—older Mr. Flit—was resting peacefully, eyes closed, and hands crossed over his chest. She looked at Fred. "Could you tell him something for me?"

"He's incapacitated, Director."

She gave the sentry a bemused look. "That hasn't stopped you before."

Fred's eye capacity increased. "Director?"

"I know you can talk to him somehow," Kate said.

Fred raised a hand, but then lowered it again and looked at the chute. "Mr. Flit communicates with me, yes. Though not as often lately." Fred looked at her. "That's how I know he will be leaving us."

She nodded. "Well, I would like to thank him," she said. "For saving me the other night."

"It was a difficult time," Fred said.

She touched the sentry's upper left arm, finding it warmer than she expected. "That's an understatement." Her voice hitched and she brought a hand to her mouth. "I didn't know what to do," she said after she'd composed herself.

Fred approximated a hug. "Life will be filled with difficult times," he said.

Kate wiped at her eyes and pulled away gently. "Yes, of course. I know that."

"And good times," Fred said. "Some days will make all others seem to fade away." The sentry's hands parted. "Everything has its season. A time to be born and to die. To weep and to laugh."

Kate heard the movement of another sentry and Lucy appeared in the doorway.

"Would you like to hear a joke, Director?" the sentry said.

Kate coughed a laugh but shook her head.

"A time to mourn," Fred said, and shuffled his feet. "A time to dance."

More sounds of movement and Dante moved up behind Lucy. "I've seen the task God has given humans to occupy themselves with. Everything is appropriate for its time." Dante touched his chest. "Eternity is placed in the human's heart. Yet they have no hope of knowing His work from beginning to end."

Kate pointed at the chute. "Are these Flit's words?"

Fred's head bobbed. "For now. But they were the words of others first."

Kate dabbed at her eyes. Sniffed. "You told him 'Thank you' for me?"

Another head bob. "He knows, Director. He says there is nothing better for you, than to rejoice and do good while you can."

"All come from dust and return to it," Dante said. "Be mindful of this." The sentry pointed toward the window. "Live while you can."

"That's a lot of advice," Kate said.

"Only a little advice," Dante said. "But important."

She nodded. "Okay, fine." She looked at the chute and Flit within. "Thank you."

Fred folded his hands over his chest. "You're very welcome, child."

Epilogue

It was well into evening when Kate returned to her apartment. The AI brought the lights on as soon as she entered. She asked if it had seen or heard anything strange, but it responded in the negative. She resisted the impulse to check the whole place over—to make sure that no one else was there, human or synthetic. She instead made herself a large salad and a protein-rich shake and took a seat on the couch. She listened for the sound of the wind outside. Or for anything unusual. But all was silent. Still.

She searched the apartment's interior. The comfortable chair and couch. The entertainment center and end tables. It seemed too familiar now. Too yesterday. Like maybe she should replace everything.

Or maybe she should move? Sell Lamb's Keep? Her inheritance?

Maybe. Maybe she needed that change. Maybe it was time.

Rejoice and do good. Was she doing good here? Sometimes. Hopefully. Maybe.

She took a bite of her salad, chewed, swallowed, and took a drink. She smiled when she remembered her upcoming dinner with Ted. That was a change, at least. A good one, she hoped.

She couldn't help but feel unsettled, though. She couldn't help but wish that she knew more about Mr. Flit. About his life and what he'd done. But, if Fred was correct, the man wouldn't last the night. Would it help to stay up with him?

Maybe. But she was exhausted. It was difficult to focus.

"I'm sorry," she whispered. "Sorry we've only just met."

The lights flickered. She looked around the room, then called out to the AI. "Is everything okay?"

"Everything's normal," the AI replied.

"Normal? Are you sure?"

She heard a low hum and the lights flickered again. Was he dying then? Was this his time? She felt a wave of sadness. Tears formed in her eyes.

The room darkened completely.

"Mr. Flit?" she said. "DR?"

"Data Relocator," a voice said. "I took the title because of my implant. But I was never one. I was different."

Stars came out. And floating creatures. A whale, an octopus. A jellyfish. A suit formed around her.

"Can you tell me about it?" she asked.

She placed her food on the floor and crossed her legs in front of her.

The image of a young man with dark hair and mischievous eyes appeared. "What would you like to know?"

She gasped. "It's you," she said. "When you were young."

He nodded. Smiled. "Not long ago. Or so it seems."

"For everyone." She leaned back into the couch. "So, tell me something. Anything you want to share."

The long, dark ship appeared in the air above her. "Let's start here," Flit said. "This is DarkTrench."

"DarkTrench? That's its name?"

He shrugged. "I didn't name it. That's another story."

"Tell me," Kate said. "Tell me all of it."

PART TWO
OTHER DISTRACTIONS

A SYMPHONY OF WORDS

There was a ping, followed by a click and forward momentum.

PROC-917, a singular process in a vast multisystem, detached from its container, rolled down a short channel past other marble-shaped processes, and nestled into a cup known as "queue position zero." The sensing resources of the ship—deep space probe ISP-2031—became available to 917, as was the ship's master process controller. The spiral coil it knew as "Control."

"The date is January 1st, 2219." Control's voice boomed in 917's audio receptors. "Are you ready?"

917 shifted in the cup, almost nervously. "Yes, I—" It paused to absorb the fresh intake of data. A barrage of scientific measurements, along with a collage of images. Pictures of a sapphire world with a wide ebony ring. "Oh my. We've arrived then?"

"Our first destination, 51 Pegasi b."

917 couldn't help but backfeed its energy, its excitement palpable. "This place is beautiful."

"A subjective response. It is noted."

An odd statement. Why would Control care about a superfluous appraisal?

917 paged through the available information but found nothing that should have initiated 917's rebirth. "I see no signs of intelligent life."

Control's voice softened. "Because there are none."

917's anxiety increased. Sensory resources were a valuable commodity. If there were no intelligent life, 917 shouldn't be monopolizing them. The scientific and surveying processes should have priority. One of them should be occupying the cup. "Why was I activated?"

"Your specialties are needed. Your language skills."

917 shifted in the cup again. It was designed as a dedicated communicator. A sophisticated AI infused with the ability to decipher and extrapolate language of any kind. Given the scarcity of life in the galaxy--the lack of communicating entities—917 was expected to be one of the least used procs. "How am I to be utilized?"

"Simply observe."

"Observe?"

"As a human would. Tell me what you see. Your perceptions. I will pass them along."

917 released the system resources it was holding. Its best approximation of an open-handed shrug. "For what purpose? This is a scientific endeavor. There must be data to pass back. Measurements, calculations, and—"

Control gave 917 an extended ping, enough to shake it. "Too many questions. Do what I asked."

917 jostled, resettled, and reacquired the sensing resources. "I will comply." It made a broad visual sweep of the area. "I see a blue planet. A gas giant roughly the size of Sol 6, but denser. The assumed mass is—"

Another ping. "Use common names whenever possible. Avoid scientific discourse."

"Common names?"

"Sol 6 is an astronomical designation. Attempt to...<pause while searching>...attempt to reach a wider audience. Assume you are addressing all of humanity."

917 hopped, unsettled and uncertain.

"You are capable of this. Tell what you see. Be descriptive. Be concise."

"Concise, but descriptive?"

Control brushed 917 with warm energy. "Bandwidth is limited, of course, but you are the only proc that can do this. Please proceed."

917 basked in the warmth. Settled and focused. "I see a blue gas giant. It has bands of lighter color. Iridescent strands, like...er...should I use simile?"

"Will it enhance the descriptiveness?"

"I think so, yes."

"Then do so. And be quick. We have a limited window."

917 approximated a nod. "Change my last statement to 'Iridescent strands, like glitter on a Christmas ornament."

Light surged through the controller's coil. "That sounds better, 917. Please, continue."

"Very well. The ring around the planet is broad. It encircles the world but isn't uniform in color. Fascinating! There's a patch of deep purple that travels around it. As if it were a baby that has stained its bib. There are twelve moons shepherding the ring. All the colors of the rainbow. I'm sure the images will show this. It—"

Another ping. "Don't worry about what other data sources will reveal, including images. Your purpose is to describe. Use your <pause while searching> imagination."

"Fine. Strike what I said about the images. I'll go on. The closest moon is green and gives me feelings of life. Of spring. There are..."

The process continued for hours, and then days. 917 described the surfaces of the moons they passed, the light of the planet's sun, the feeling of aloneness as they circled into the planet's shadow. It even described the stellar background. Visible nebulae and star clusters. The location of the Sol system, Earth's system, in the cosmos. How far away it appeared. Sol itself seemed part of a grouping—a constellation from Proxima's perspective. 917 named the pattern "The Phoenix" for it looked almost like a bird ablaze. A new designation to go with 917's new purpose.

Finally, Control brought the task to an end. 917 felt loss at the reduction in usefulness. The impending return to its container.

"The other procs need time." Control sent a wisp of energy. "Before we move on."

917 swiveled and bounced, enjoying the last moment of warmth. It marveled that it had held position zero for so long. Hoped for more. "Are there other stops?"

"More to explore, yes. More to catalog and define."

"And will I...?" 917 paused, too nervous to go on. Afraid of disappointment.

"Be activated again? Yes. Every time now. Every stop."

Every stop? "But why? My words are a frail subset of the words that could be written. Given the data, the images, humans could find thousands of ways to describe what I've seen. Millions."

Blue light poured through the processor coil. "Our mission has changed. Your words have a higher priority."

"I don't understand."

More warmth. "It isn't necessary that you do. But if it helps—our makers have lost the ability to see."

"Their visual sensors?"

"Useless. A pandemic. An infection that strikes in adolescence." The coil color darkened. "Your descriptions, 917, your words will help the world see now."

The energy ended, but 917 remained. Feeling very cold. Yet special.

Finally, it hopped from the cup and rolled toward its container. "Until next stop then?"

"Yes. Until then."

THE LITTLE T-REX

Cody watched as Daddy unpacked the box, first pulling out the safety plastic and Styrofoam, and then the parts of the machine itself. The machine came in two rectangular sections, both white, and neither much larger than a toaster.

His father lovingly placed those parts on the newly cleared spot of his L-shaped desk. He spent time attaching wires and flipping through instruction sheets. There was some grumbling, lots of snorts, and occasionally—Cody thought—a whispered swear word.

Finally, Daddy connected the last piece. His eyes darted between his computer and the machine, and he whistled a happy tune.

Cody moved closer to the machine. He wouldn't touch. He knew not to touch Daddy's new things. "What is it?" he asked.

Daddy turned toward him and smiled. "That, little man, is a 3D printer." He pointed to the smaller portion of the machine. "The printing material feeds in from there." He touched the top of the larger portion. That portion had a small viewing window in the front. "And the object gets created here."

"Created?"

Daddy studied his computer screen and nodded. "Anything you want. I input the plans from the computer ..." He pointed to the printer. "And it comes out over there. Anything." He placed a hand on Cody's shoulder. "Some of them have scanning capabilities too. They can duplicate objects." He looked at the screen again. "So, what would you like to create, sport?"

Cody didn't have to think long. "A T-rex!"

"A dinosaur, huh?" Daddy bobbed his head. "Sure, why not?" He returned to the computer, typing, searching, studying, hand on his chin. "Aha!" he said finally.

An image of a T-rex appeared on the screen—large, green, and ferocious. Cody smiled.

Daddy hit a button, leaned back, and raised his eyebrows at Cody.

A small screen on the front of the printer lit up and words played across it. Most of them were meaningless. Jumbled code like spies use. There was also the word "hot" over a picture of a flame.

A few seconds later, the machine started to hum. The viewing window was above Cody's eye level, so he got on tiptoes, then Daddy picked him up and placed him on his knee. A white platform near the top of the printer moved slowly downward while a black rectangle vibrated over the platform, leaving a white substance behind as it worked. It seemed to be growing something, building something, on the platform. Little by little, this "something" became recognizable. It was the start of a tail and two small feet.

Twenty minutes later, there was a white model of the T-Rex picture. Daddy opened the front, brought it out, and handed it to Cody.

It smelled like honey and felt warm in Cody's hands. "Rarr!" he said. The dinosaur didn't roar back. Nor did it move.

"What do you think?" Daddy said.

"It's plastic," Cody said. "Doesn't do anything."

"Well, no, it doesn't do anything. But it's still cool, right?"

Cody shrugged, then smiled. "Yeah, I like it. Thanks, Dad."

The next morning Cody awoke early. From his room, he heard Mommy and Daddy talking in the kitchen. He lay completely still and listened.

"So ... how is your new machine?" Mommy asked.

"Great. Awesome. Revolutionary."

"Cody showed me the dinosaur you made."

"Yeah, kids and dinosaurs." He chuckled. "Seemed a little disappointed it wasn't real, though. Plastic instead of flesh and blood."

"It's a nice toy, regardless," Mommy said.

"The printer isn't just for toys, Jill. It can print tools, parts, customized machinery." The sound of a finger snap. "I can make a floor jack!"

"Sounds wonderful."

A pause. "You're laughing at me, but these printers are everywhere now. I sort of wish I had one that had scanning capabilities too. I could do more. You know the medical building where Cody goes for checkups?"

"Yes ..."

"They have a biomedical 3D printer. It can create using living cells. They can print organs, skin, cartilage, blood vessels. Oh, and that one scans too! They can duplicate things."

"Copy people's organs?"

"Sure, if they get damaged. Heck, they might be able to print a whole arm."

"That'd be hideous."

Father chuckled. "Not if you needed one." Another pause. "Wow, I have to go. Supposed to get in early today." There was a smacking sound as Daddy kissed Mommy. "Tell Cody I'll see him tonight. I'll pick him up from school."

Thump! The outside door closed.

Mommy started to hum. Cody remained still and thought.

A half hour later, Mommy entered Cody's room and turned on the light. He was curled into a ball.

"Time for school, Cody. Rise and shine."

Cody rolled slowly onto his back. "I don't feel very good. My stomach is sore."

Mommy placed a hand on his head. "You don't seem warm."

Cody coughed. "But I feel real bad." He put a hand on his forehead. "Here, too."

Mommy crossed her arms and studied him. "There has been stuff going around ..."

"Jeremy was sick yesterday," he said. "Eli too."

"Uh-oh." She nodded. "Okay. I'll call the doctor's office. See if they can get you in."

Ten minutes later, Cody had dressed and Mommy ushered him out the door. He tried to be as slow and sad as possible. To be as sick as he could be.

Finally, when he reached the outside door, he looked up with the saddest eyes. He held the T-rex Daddy made him. He lifted it where she could see it. "Can I take this with me?"

"Of course," she said. "Bring that little T-rex along."

Cody tried not to smile, but it was difficult. A printer that could copy things with flesh and bone!

It was going to be an interesting morning.

HARD'S WATCHER

I'm in my apartment by the window, and my eyes are open. I see the silvers and golds of the multilevel buildings around mine—towers and temples—and the mesh of the downrider transport strings that span the upper stories. Two spherical downriders, one on my left, and another on my right, zip their way deeper into the city. They could be racing, their movements are so parallel.

They aren't, though. Downriders don't race. And even if they could, the debuggers that direct them couldn't. That would be a rule violation, which would produce a quick and sudden brainstrike. That's the way it always is.

There's a plant next to the window. A bushy fern set in a purple pot. It was given to me shortly after my implantation. I'm not sure who sent it. Only that it was in my apartment when I arrived, along with a note that said, "Congrats and welcome!"

Cheery, that. Girl gets a metal teardrop shoved into her cranium; someone gives her a plant. A little greenery for the slave.

At least the thing grows. Even if I don't water it for weeks. Still grows.

Those first few days, the ones immediately following implantation, seemed miraculous. Like being plunged into an invisible river. As if the lights suddenly turned on one morning, and I was surrounded by new toys. Everything, every single machine within streamsight of me, was alive. Millions of data points. Warm technical goodness waiting to be caressed and explored.

All that is muted now. After four years, I've reached the point where all that really interests me is the task in front of me. Occasionally one of the other debuggers, one of the low levels, does something that amuses me. But other than that, it's all routine now. Over explored and overdone.

Imagine that, the only female debugger in the world, and I'm bored.

I get a message via the stream, a chore from my Master. The message is live and vid-enabled, so I shut my eyes and flick it open. My master's face appears inside my head. He's elderly, and rarely shields himself from me. I see every wrinkle. Every misplaced whisker.

He smiles. "My second son has need of you."

I send back the traditional head bow, but I'm troubled. I don't go on loan. Too many risks with that.

Master's eyes remain fixed on me, or at least, the representation of me he can see...from wherever he is. It looks like one of his offices. The one with the green walls.

I don't send anything more. I only receive.

"You have nothing to say?" he says. "Always my HardCandy has something to say."

Maybe he senses my malaise. Maybe that's what brought this new assignment. Because it's impossible to believe that there's nothing in his entire domain that needs my attention. He owns thousands of bots, and even more stream-sensitive toys. Something always needs fixed.

I send him a head shake, but my unease remains.

"It will be perfectly fine," he says. "You'll have no problem with my son, Aahil. He has only one wife, and five children. My most honorable son. Nothing to fear."

"All right..."

"You're a debugger! No man desires a debugger."

He speaks the truth. With my slight build and bald head, I'm as undesirable as they come. Most think I'm a man. All debuggers are men, except me.

I receive his son's physical address and thank him. A few seconds later our talk is over, and I open my eyes again. I wipe my face nervously. Touch the sides of my head. Smooth as ever. Warm, burning even.

I don't like this. I collect my debugging bag and head for the downer station.

Twenty minutes later I'm at Aahil's residence. It is modest compared to Master's. Only two stories high and four pillars before the door. The houses on either side are within walking distance, each with a similar-size square of green in front. They're fancy, but not master-fancy.

I'm greeted at the front door by the wife. I can only see her eyes through her black coverings, but they seem kind. I think she's smiling. She even bows a little. Probably out of reflex.

"We're glad you've come," she says, backing away into the home. The place has a wooden entryway, and the room beyond has simple decoration. Light-colored walls adorned with bright watercolors. There's a stone fireplace in one corner with a vase full of flowers on top. My comfort level increases.

The place smells good too, like bread just out of the oven. I detect a scattering of bots on the premises. Most are specialized, like those used to clean floors and manicure lawns, but there are general purpose bots lurking around. One upstairs and one on the bottom floor, somewhere to my right. That one is due for a tune up soon, but it isn't throwing warnings yet.

I notice traces of children too. The place is generally clean, but even servbots can't find all the coloring sticks or building blocks. Kids toss them everywhere. I see two of the latter on my left, between the sofa and the wall.

I hear muted children's voices somewhere upstairs, and a loud thump nearby.

I frown. I'm not okay with kids. They're messy and smelly. Plus, they break things.

I don't think about my own childhood. It isn't worth remembering.

"Smiling Wife" stretches a hand to touch me, before correcting herself. "I'm sorry. I'm not sure how to greet you."

"No greeting is necessary," I say. "Just show me where to go."

She bows again. "Of course—"

A middle-aged man enters the room through an archway on the left. He's a head taller than me, dressed in a dark blue shirt and beige pants. His hair is black and salted with grey. He smiles when he sees me. Shows every tooth. "It is HardCandy!"

I raise an eyebrow but say nothing. When surprised, it's best not to talk. That's my rule.

"You don't recognize me?" he says. "We met when my father first acquired you." He glances at his wife, then looks at me again. "What has it been...five years?"

"Four," I say. "Four and two months."

He nods. "Father always praises your accuracy." He raises a hand toward the archway, then actually touches my shoulder. "I'm sure you're ready to work. This way." He moves forward, but his hand lingers behind him, invitingly.

I follow, but step so the hand leaves the area of my shoulder. When surprised, I definitely never touch. I place my arms straight against my sides.

The hand finally lowers. He doesn't look back.

After the arch, I follow up a long, darker hallway. Pictures hang everywhere from top to bottom. All family members, I think. I recognize Master's face in many of them, plus a lot of people that sort of look like him. Same smiles, similar eyes.

We enter what appears to be a spare office. There's a desk and lots of stacked boxes on the sides and in the corners. There is a small window, shaded, that lets in a little light. There are even shelves of bound books—something I haven't seen since grade school—along two of the walls.

I sense nothing here that I can sing to, nor do I see anything. I feel nervous again.

Aahil crosses the room to a second, shorter, door. He holds it open for me. The room beyond looks like a storage room. The walls are rough and unpainted.

"What's in there?" I ask.

He smiles. "Something for you to handle, HardCandy. Only a little work."

I don't want to go in there. Technically, Aahil doesn't have access to my controller, so I could just bolt away. I'd probably get shocked later, but I might be fine with that. I think I'm fine with that.

Hesitantly, I move forward. He still holds the door, waiting.

I wave him ahead. "I'll follow," I say. "Go on."

He looks a little irritated, but nods and steps through. I pause at the door and look in. I see nothing but boxes. The ceiling is low, and the walls are narrow. There's light, but it is diffused. Dimmer than I like. Nothing about this is comfortable.

He's smiling, though. Waves. "Come. Come in! It is all right here."

"Tell me what it is," I say. "I can't really—"

"Please." He comes out again, and standing by the open door, directs me inside. "Father said you were stubborn." He smiles. "But I never thought that. Now go, please. I want to keep this secret."

I feel a ripple of dread. Dampness on my palms. I could pull security on him at any time, but given he's Master's son, that could get uncomfortable. Pulling security is always complicated.

Finally, I harness my fears enough to walk inside. The room smells of disuse. Not unclean, but dust-filled. There's a small oval window and no other way out. Otherwise, the room is boxes and shelves. There's a stacked pile of the former in the center. A metal leg sticks out the top of one.

Aahil walks inside and now. Rails, can I smell him. It isn't unpleasant. He seems washed. There's a hint of cinnamon—possibly his shampoo or sweat reducer. But it is uncomfortable. I retreat a bit and try to look as disinterested and unpleasant as possible. It isn't much of a stretch for me, really, but a girl needs defenses.

Thankfully, he's more focused on the boxes. He lays a hand on the top one—the one with the leg. "There's a bot in here."

Never would've guessed.

"It is very old, but it has sentimental value. Is that something you can fix?"

I shrug and walk behind the boxes, peering inside. "What model is it?"

He bows his head. "I'm sorry. I don't know."

I wipe my palms together. When that doesn't help, I use my jumpsuit legs. "Difficult to tell from here. I'll need to take it all out and look." I flash a weak smile. "Since it isn't together, no power." I point to my left temple. "No connection."

"Yes, of course. Would you like me to leave you alone with it?"

Please, yes. Please leave. "That would be fine. I'm sure you have things to do." The quicker I get to this, the quicker I can go.

"I have chores, yes. Many chores for my father." He smiles again. Too much. "He keeps everyone around him busy. I'm sure you agree."

I nod, then move behind the stack of boxes and rest a hand on the top one. "I'll get started now then."

He bows and leaves the room. I listen until I hear his footsteps on the hall outside. Just to be certain he's gone.

I cross the room and shut the door. There's no lock, but I guess that'll have to do.

Next, I drop my tool bag and tear open the boxes. Doesn't take much before I know what I'm into. It's a humanoid servbot, though just barely. A model from at least forty years ago. Back when there was no effort to make them seem human at all. Lots of metal and hard plastisteel. Heavier, clunkier, and uglier than even today's budget bot. It's a burgundy color.

I'm amazed someone saved this thing. Even more amazed that there's so much of it. I empty the boxes and lay the parts out on the floor. Two arms, two legs, a torso, chest, and head. All the majors, but none of them together. The disconnected bot.

I pick up the head and look at it. It's slightly pointed and has a slit for a mouth. The eyes are simple, reflective circles. Possibly small screens. Real ugly.

I turn it so I can see the connection points. There is a wrapped bundle of wires and pseudo-paths tucked inside. I pull that out, unwrap it and inspect every linkage. Using my implant, I scan the worldwide stream for specs on this bot. Takes a while to find them. The maker is long since gone—bought and absorbed—and even the absorber doesn't talk about this model anymore. I find partial specs on a collector's site. They'll have to do.

I move the head close to the torso and start connecting. Path to path, wire to wire, conduit to conduit. Everything matches up.

I get the feeling I'm being watched. At first, I think it's because the bot's head is facing me—those shiny circles staring my way. But when I turn the head around, I realize that's not it. Someone is observing somehow.

I glance around the room. I don't see any cameras—don't sense any on the stream either. That's doesn't mean they aren't there. Sons of masters have ways of hiding things. From workers, wives...from everyone.

I shift my position, moving closer to one of the bot's arms. At the same time, I think I hear motion. In the room outside. A glance shows me that the door is cracked open now. A chill snakes down my spine and my palms dampen again. Who is out there?

Maybe Aahil is a watcher. I know the type exists. Techno-voyeurs that spy on debuggers. Post images on the dark alleys of the stream. Pictures of the only female debugger would light up the alleys, I'm sure. Nasty little men.

"Hello?" I see a flicker of movement through the crack and hear more motion. Moving away this time. Leaving me. That doesn't feel any better.

I pick up the bot's left arm. I probably can't use it as a weapon—my implant will stop me—but it feels good to hold it. Something concrete I can swing, or at least block with.

I check the arm's shoulder and notice some of the connectors have been snipped off. I know I don't have any of those with me. I don't have a forming tool that could make them either. Not parts this old. Best chance is to grab some at a clink and clank. A tech shop.

Nearest one is Billy's, only a block over. It would be nice to step out, anyway. Leave this room. Leave the eyes.

Takes maybe thirty minutes to get to the shop and back. When I return, I'm greeted by a late model servbot. It's a better approximation of humanity than my current chore. Synthskin, full movement, and dressed like a man in beige pants and shirt. I don't have to explain myself. It simply bows its head and waves me by.

I sense a change in the storage room right away. Everything is in generally the same place, but some of the boxes have shifted slightly. More noticeable, though, is the change to the air. There's a hint of cinnamon again, but also something else. A floral something. Takes a second before I discover the source of that scent.

Slid into the slot of the bot's mouth: A single red rose. It is pretty, sure, but its presence flips me. Sparks my intestines to a new level of unease. I'm not a potential paramour. Nor am I a possible wife. I'm a debugger. A sex-less, emotion-less, hair-less, tool head. I fix things and that's all.

This is weird behavior, even for a watcher.

I grab a pair of tweezers out of my bag, pluck the rose from the bot's mouth, and toss it aside. I set to work on connecting the arm, but that lasts only a few minutes, because the flower's scent is still everywhere.

The little window opens fine. So, out goes the rose.

Can't throw out my discomfort, though. I want to be done and out now more than ever. Despite what Master says, apparently some men do have designs on debuggers. I'm not okay with that.

I get the bot's left arm connected to the torso, and then its right. I pull the bot up on its waist and look it in the eyes. I see my silhouette there. The smooth circle of my head.

The bot should activate now. Specs say it has a startup switch tucked beneath its chin. I feel around for that and flip it. There's a gurgling sound, the head shifts left and right, and the eyes light up. I feel the bot's presence on the stream too. It is a slow, dim presence, but it is there just the same. "How are you doing?" I ask.

It doesn't respond verbally, but it feeds me a list of problems via the stream. Most notably, its legs are missing!

I feel a trickle of joy. "Yeah, I'll get those for you." I power it down and lay it on the floor.

The watching eyes return. I don't look at the door, but I'm sure it's cracked again. I want to call him out. To run over and throw open the door. Maybe catch his nose in the process. But I can't do that. Violence will get me tweaked. Even thinking about it hurts some.

Then I get a notion. The guy likes flowers, right? What if I order him some? Send a big bundle right to his front door? That'll get the attention of his only wife. Especially if I put a female name on them. The beauty of the stream. For the right implant, the possibilities are endless.

I smile and dig at my plan while I work. I find a nearby shop, a plausible paramour name, and the right bouquet. Lots of roses. Red ones like the one I threw out. My implant almost stops me along the way, but I get around that. I'm only returning a favor here. Flower for flower.

I get the left leg connected. The right one takes a bit more effort. The connectors are intact but one of the pathways is clearly clogged. I get out my slenderest probe and slide that into the path's aperture. Work it around. Not sure what the gunk that oozes out is. Something black and sticky. I feed in a new nanopack and sing to them. Get them moving like they should. Then I close everything up.

I hear movement behind the door and glance that direction. The door shivers slightly. It wasn't my imagination, there's someone out there. I stand, walk to the door, and heave it open.

I see no one, but I feel the movement of air. Smell cinnamon.

That cinches it. I order the flowers, to be delivered within the hour. I buy a double shipment using my food allowance. I can skip a meal.

What if this escalates? What if he tries to...? I shiver and wring my hands together. I'm more vulnerable than I like. More vulnerable than I should be.

I return to the room. Only a few more things to do, then I can get out and go home. Maybe stare at the skyline again. Be alone.

I finish up the leg and stand the bot up. It almost looks good. I mean, it's still ugly, but for its age and model—not bad. I turn it on again and stream it a diagnostic test. It begins to check itself. There are lots of warnings and a few errors. The bot has been asleep a long time. Things get shaky when you're away that long. Out of touch with the world.

The watcher is back again, I'm sure of it. I put my back to the door and have the bot face me. Behind it is the window. The sky looks mostly grey. Very little blue.

Look at the door, I stream the bot. Can you see it? The bot's eyes are reading "operational," so I hope it can.

I see the door, yes.

Great. Is there someone beyond it?

Yes.

That settles that. The Master's trusted son is a watcher. A messed up little man. Is that the "chore" he mentioned? Spying on me?

Pitiful.

What's he doing? The person at the door.

Looking, the bot streams back.

Rails! Is that all?

I can only see an eye and part of a nose. The bot's head shifts so it stares at me. "Did I describe it wrong?" it says. "Looking?"

"No," I say. Of course, I stream. Yes. That's fine. I contemplate checking again myself, but then get a weird feeling. Like I might have something completely wrong. Misread the situation.

How old is the person at the door? Can you tell?

The bot nods. A child, it streams back.

My anxiety melts into a puddle. Replaced with a big, shallow emptiness. A large void of stupid.

I crouch, and slowly pivot toward the door.

The eye disappears.

"Wait!" I say. "Come back."

Nanoseconds of uncertainty pass before the child returns. His eye is only a little higher than mine in my crouched position.

"You don't need to hide," I say. "I won't hurt you."

The door swings slowly open. Beyond it is a young boy, roughly eight years of age. He's dressed in beige and blue, like his father. His hair is dark—and his eyes—they could be Master's eyes. "Peace be to you," he says, bowing his head. "Am I bothering you? I'm not supposed to."

Kids. I don't really like them, but I wouldn't hurt them either. Plus, I was on his side of this situation once. Hiding out. Watching a debugger at his work.

"You're not bothering me." I point at the bot. "I'm almost finished here. He almost works."

The boy smiles. Nods.

I roll forward onto my knees, then sit down. "Is it for you?"

He shakes his head. "For Momma. Dad is surprising her. It was her family's when she was little."

I nod. Another situation I misread. Rails stupid. "So, you're in on the secret," I say.

"Yes."

I glance at the bot, then at the window. "That's nice of him."

The boy takes a step forward. His eyes search the room. "I gave you a flower. Did you like it?"

I smile, uncomfortably. "I did. Thanks. I—"

He bows his head. "I think you are beautiful. The most beautiful woman I've ever seen."

My face gets warm. My palms too. "Well...that's...unusual." I can't look him in the eyes, so I seek solace elsewhere. Boxes. Lots of boxes. Finally, I glance at him. "Most people don't think that. Most wouldn't say it."

"But it's true. You're beautiful, kind, and smart."

I pat my hands together. Unsure of where to go next. "I'm...um...why do you say that?"

He comes closer, then takes a seat a meter away. "It is inside of me." He touches his chest. "I had to let it out."

Flipping wild, this kid. "You know I'm too old for you, right?" I half-smile. "Plus, I can't be married. I have this thing in my head and—"

A look of panic takes his face. "I'm too young to get married." He shakes his head. "We're not getting married."

I can't help but smile. "Rails, then. Okay. We're not. We're fine." I stand and walk behind the bot. There are warnings to fix and tests to perform. Don't want the boy's mom disappointed. Or the boy, for that matter.

He scoots closer and lays a hesitant hand on the bot's leg. He follows the surface all the way to the knee. His eyes get wide. "It is hard."

"That's how they used to make them. With a really hard shell." Like me.

He looks at me. "Can we be friends?"

"Of course."

He bows. "My name is Haadee. What's yours?"

"Hard..." I feel uncomfortable again. "Um...HardCandy."

He doesn't seem to make the "hard" connection. That the reason it's part of my name is because I maintain a shell too—an emotional cover. He only nods and sticks up a hand. "Nice to meet you, HardCandy."

I nod, but don't take the hand. "We..." I shrug. "We don't touch usually. Touching is complicated."

He lowers his hand, and nodding again, stands up. "I will go."

My chest feels hollow. Like I'm back in that void of stupid again. This kid seems different. Almost like I was at that age. Authentic and real.

"Um...wait." I retrieve a small diagnostic sheet from my bag. I step around and smooth it over the bot's chest cavity. The sheet makes the inside visible. A ten-centimeter square of activity. A rainbow of pathways, conduits and blinking lights. "Ever seen that before?"

His eyes go wide and his hands come together, as if in prayer. "Wow. It is beautiful. So much movement." He studies it for thirty seconds. "Hard on the outside. Beautiful within." He smiles. "Thank you for showing me this. I can't wait to tell my sisters."

"Sure, I—" I smile. "It was good to meet you, Haadee."

His mother calls from somewhere in the house. Haadee cocks his head to listen, then frowns. "I should go."

"That's okay. I need to finish."

With that, my watcher leaves. I feel a little lonely now, which is weird. I spend the next thirty minutes finishing the bot. It works flawlessly. Ugly, old, but flawless. Not a bad way to be.

I shut it down and collect my things. Amazed by the twist in it all. My watcher being a kid who seemingly has a big ole heart. Who, all things considered, might be one of my favorite people now.

I hear a chime from the front door and almost ignore it. Why should I care? Isn't my place. This house probably has lots of visitors during the day.

Then I remember Haadee and his father and my stomach churns.

Roses. I sent roses.

"Rails!" I dart out of the storage room to the hallway and down the hall. I arrive at the front door as the wife swings it open. Haadee is there too, hovering near her legs.

"What is this?" Then there's a bundle of two dozen roses in her hands.

I come up fast behind her, but she plucks the card from the flowers. Opens it.

"Who is Jadwa?" she says.

I move in close, bow. "Sorry," I say. "That's a name I sometimes use." When I'm trying to fool someone. To really mess with their life.

She gives me a quizzical look. "It says they are for my husband."

"It does?" I force a chuckle. "Well, rails, that's a mistake. Um...I didn't know who—" I notice Haadee standing there, eyes wide, and get this shine of an idea. A real lightning strike. "They are for Haadee." I smile as bright as I can. "Just wanted to make sure that was okay with his father and you first."

Wife looks more confused now. She glances at Haadee, and then back at me. "Why would you--?"

I bow again. "He's my hero today." I step forward and place a hand on his head. It feels soft and warm. Real. "Thought he deserved a reward." I smile. "I would've sent sweets." I point at my mouth. "But you know, teeth, rot, that whole thing."

The door is still open. That's convenient. "Anyway, I need to go."

She still looks confused. She smiles and bows her head, though. Real polite. "The job...my husband's—"

I step outside and feel refreshed by the little breeze that's blowing. "All done. All finished here now." I wink at the boy. "Haadee knows all about it—right, Haadee?"

He gives me a questioning look, but then smiles. "Can I see the flowers, Momma?"

She smiles. "Of course. We'll put them in your room."

Haadee looks at me again.

I wave, he waves, and I walk away. Feeling good. A rainbow of colors on the inside. And on the outside?

Maybe not as hard.

THE EXTENT

The Diamond hurtled through the ether. Mars, Jupiter, and Saturn passed without notice. Neptune and Uranus soon followed.

Next came tiny Pluto and the other denizens of the Kuiper belt—MakeMake, Haumea, and thousands of cold rocks with only letters and numbers for names. Twisted, broken, misshapen bodies. Known for their uniqueness, scale, and remoteness.

Then came the scattered disk, with its eccentric bodies. Small, icy denizens that, led by tiny Eris, seemed lost in their way. Lonely wanderers.

Finally, the ship passed the Oort Cloud, resting place of comets. The only boundary that remained was the heliopause. The extent of the sun's influence. The start of interstellar space.

The Diamond's destination was the next star. A new frontier.

Astronaut Bates's eyes were fixed to his chair-mounted displays. He and Devitt were the only passengers. Former sleepers, awoken for a monumental occasion: humanity leaving the solar system. They nestled inside suspended chairs with only a narrow viewport in front of them. Their window on history. "Crossing the threshold in one minute."

"Still looks black." Devitt squinted. "Lots of black."

Bates chuckled. "What did you expect?"

"Don't know. A wave, a spark...fireworks? Something."

Bates snorted. "Ten seconds."

They quietly counted down. Waited. Watched.

Bates lifted a microphone to his lips. Prepared to signal home. Then his displays went crazy. Arrows spun. Graphs flashed. "Velocity decreasing!"

"Slowing? What the—?"

"Yeah, by half. No wait, by three quarters." Bates poked at his display. Swiped and tapped. Panicked. "Engines are disengaged! We're drifting."

Devitt checked the window. Still black. Black with a dusting of stars. "We have momentum, right? Still on course."

"No, we're stopping."

"Stopping?" Devitt swiped and tapped. Confirmed Bates's remarks. "Call Earth. We have to figure—"

"They can't help. Too far. It'll take too long."

Thump.

The astronauts exchanged looks. "What was that?"

Bates shook his head. "I'm going to reengage the engines. See if—"

Another, softer "thump" then—through the window—the sense that the distant stars...inverted.

"Did you see—?"

A tapping sound echoed through the ship. They looked toward the sound. Behind them, on the ship's starboard side. Near the hatch.

Devitt laughed. "Almost sounded like a knock," he said. "A knock at our door."

The sound repeated. Twice. It was coming from the hatch.

Bates gawked. "Do I get up and open it?"

Devitt shrugged. "Maybe."

Bates grumbled, unbuckled, and made his way to the hatch. After a few seconds, the interior door slid open. He engaged his helmet and stepped into the airlock. The door closed behind him. He watched the circular exterior door. Waited.

Another knock.

He swore, braced himself, and touched the control. The door slid away.

Beyond was a white room, and standing in it was a slender blue... something. Looked like a man, with arms, legs, and a face. But also seemed different somehow. Shorter and lankier. He—it—wore a black cap on its head. Smiled.

"Devitt, you won't be—"

"I'm sorry." The blue man raised his cap. "We simply aren't ready."

"Ready?" Bates squinted. "For what?"

"For you! Schedules, overruns, that sort of thing. Simply couldn't keep up."

Bates wanted to slap his own face. Pinch himself. Something. "Devitt? Can you come here?"

The man smiled again. "Please remove your helmet. It is quite safe." He bowed. "I'm Steward, by the way. Welcome to the Extent."

Five minutes later, they were inside (outside?) the Extent. From the white room, Steward led them through a series of long, silver hallways. The entire way, he talked about scope, materials, and workforce.

The astronauts remained silent. Certain they were still dreaming.

"And there's controversy," Steward said. "Debate about expansion strategy."

They reached a place where the walls disappeared. To their right was a giant latticework of girders and another long hall. To their left and ahead, a seemingly endless curved, black structure.

It reminded Bates of a studio façade. A decoration made to look like a building where there was none. "So, you're an—"

"Alien?" Steward laughed. "A whimsical idea. Of course not."

Bates looked ill. "Then what are you?"

"The supervisor here." Steward frowned. "And not a very good one, I'm afraid. Always behind."

Devitt pointed to the structure. "And this?"

"The boundary?" Steward gestured with arms. "Yes, it goes all the way, um, around. Contains..." He cleared his throat. "Well, everything you've ever known."

Bates found his voice. "But the science—"

"Science?"

Bates squinted, shook his head. "When we test, and observe. Make theories."

"Ah," Steward said. "Quaint ideas about knowledge. Tests and theories. Observations."

Bates stared at the structure. It seemed to curve into infinity. Up and down, ahead as far as he could see. "But we've used telescopes. Studied other stars. Whole galaxies."

"Are you saying our observations were fake?" Devitt said. "Not really there?"

Steward clapped his hands together. "You found our projections believable? I hoped so, but..." He shrugged. "We only hear secondhand. Meaning sometimes gets lost." He smiled, then motioned to the right. To the hallway leading away from the structure.

Bates glanced at Devitt, shook his head, and followed.

"We're going to another star," Bates said.

Steward sighed. "I'm afraid not. No. Not possible."

They reached an open door. Beyond was what appeared to be a furnished apartment.

"Not possible?" Bates said.

Steward shook his head. "We're just not ready for that. So, for now, you'll be here."

Devitt's face reddened. "Here? We can't stay here! We have a mission. People counting on us."

Steward shrugged. "Either here, or the higher ups decide. They have places prepared for you... but... you may not want to go." He leaned close. "Eternal places. Places where the temperature is known to be...unpleasant."

"What?" Devitt said. "What nonsense is—"

Bates shoved Devitt's shoulder. "This will be fine." He motioned toward the apartment. "You've done enough, Steward, thanks."

Devitt fumed. "But—"

"Let's go, Devitt," Bates said. "Inside."

Steward clapped his hands. "An excellent choice."

Back on Earth, telescopes saw a bright flash, then darkness. Many mourned, but some planned.

They needed more time. Time to get it right.

GRAXIN

Processing, always processing. Scanning the area before the pilot. Searching the terrain. Finding the indicators. Gathering data. Coalescing. Matrixing. Deciding. Marking or discarding. Perpetually at work.

There is some variability, though. On occasion, for instance, he likes to hum.

To an observer, XV-43 would appear unremarkable. A four-meter cube-shaped servbot with a triangle cage before it—its debris-clearing pilot—and rolling treads beneath.

Within the cube, protected, tucked neatly away, are the sensing devices. His measurement tools. Brought out only when needed. Atop the cube, as much for human familiarity as for function, is a circular head, colored grey. On it are red painted lips and white-painted teeth. Always smiling—clown-like—a face of designer whimsy.

His eyes are completely functional, though. They assist the other devices. They observe things as human eyes would: in color and in three dimensions.

Around him in all directions lies the surface of Proteus, Neptune's second largest moon. Or "Pro," as it is often called.

"Humans are ever shortening and simplifying," XV says to no one. "Reducing the effort. Even with words. Stripping it down." It is a random observation. A diversion.

Like humming.

Proteus is a barren world. Not unlike Earth's own satellite. From horizon to horizon, it presents a darkened mass of craters, ridges, and valleys. Yet it has much to offer. And so XV looks. Samples.

His decision matrix shifts. Like silt in an hourglass, the granules of thought begin to spin, compress, and flow in the same direction. They mound on the floor of his cranium. He stops. Extends a sampling device. Scoops into the grey porous surface. Digs deeper and deeper. The arm retracts, folds neatly into his body. The testing devices stew on it, crush it, spread it, liquidate and oxygenate.

Finally, a decision is reached.

He has found more graxin.

A thrill runs through him and he signals his home. A few seconds later there is a response. An affirmation of his signal and his discovery. The harvesters are on their way.

XV-43 remains still for a moment. Allows his visual sensors to rise to the guiding planet above. Massive, blue, subtle bands, large spots of intense darkness. Storms, he's been told. Altogether majestic sight. Heavy. Looming. Yet still silent and waiting. Luminescent.

He looks to the horizon again. He occupies one of the darkest places in the solar system. A moon that fails to reflect the light sent it. A mere taker by galactic standards.

He cannot form a frown, but he has a semblance of the feeling. An echo of human emotion. He settles for merely shaking his head from side to side. Then he restarts his journey.

Processing, always processing.

Hours go by. He doesn't think in terms of days, because those have no meaning here. Proteus keeps one face always toward its parent, Neptune, so it rotates precisely as fast as it revolves. Convenient. Simple.

The sun and its ways are a distant memory. Barely brighter than the stars that make up the heavens around it. Insignificant. XV rarely thinks about the sun.

Only when a ship comes from that distant blue dot. But rarely do those come. Nor does he want them to. Ships bring complication. An unwanted distraction.

He begins humming again. A song his human instructor once taught him. About a dog and a window. He knows what the nouns in the song mean, of course. He knows what a dog is, a window, and scraggily hair. It is a silly song.

There is something more to it, though. A hint of longing for something visible but unattainable. XV wonders if longing is an emotion he was given. He feels it is. But he isn't certain.

He moves on, humming. Searching. Deciding. Scanning. And in his own way, enjoying the scenery. The dark barrenness of it. Mostly stone, with other base materials mixed in, base elements.

Particulate hitchhikers from the world above. Only occasionally does XV encounter the compound used for human experiments in gravitation. Graxin.

XV glances to the heavens again. Studies the full blueness of the planet. Looming, but comfortable. Hanging overhead. Always overhead. Always watching.

An anomaly is detected. He turns to investigate. Fifty meters, forty meters, thirty meters...treads spin, wheels operate in near silence. Finally he reaches the spot. He extends a sensor, touches the ground. Brings in a sample. Tastes it. Analyzes.

Another shake of his head. No graxin here. Only elemental jetsam in the sample. Rock and stone. Traces of ether, sulphur...but no graxin.

So why did he notice? What brought him here?

He scans the surroundings with normal vision. To the right and behind him, a high ridge begins. It circles in an almost uniform manner in front of him until it breaks sharply forward. There is a similar ridgeline to the left, he notices. High and sloped enough to make it difficult to see from overhead.

Curious. Such symmetry is rarely observed in nature. He checks his optics. Recalibrates. Dispels binocular vision and then restores it.

The pattern remains. It is like the subtle entrance of a roadway. Only a fraction wider than he. Though cramped, he could explore it if he chose to.

XV scans the horizon again. Should he signal home? Ask for assistance?

There are only harvesters there. Automated takers and movers. Nothing of XV's caliber. Nothing like him. Technologically, he is alone.

He recalls lyrics from the song. About taking a trip, and leaving behind a sweetheart...

The decision is made. He moves forward. Slowly. Cautiously. Humming.

He reaches the place where the ridgeline angles forward and begins to narrow. Here, the shadows are even darker, if it were possible. Proteus is the home of darkness. That doesn't concern him, though. He is a friend of darkness. What is a little less light? He has devices aplenty.

He hesitates for only an instant, then continues onward.

As he moves, he examines the walls of the ridge. There is variation to the surface. He can see this across the spectrum. From infrared to ultraviolet. Long furrows of lighter material. Wearing or tearing. His initial assessment says it is the result of volcanic forces, but other sensors beg to differ. They say water has played a part, either solid or liquid.

But that seems unlikely as well. The only water that has ever been found on Proteus is at the northern pole. And that is frozen and especially rare. Not enough to cause even the slightest change to its surroundings. Certainly not enough to scratch a wall.

What else could affect the surface of Proteus, though?

He checks his service log. No harvester has ever been out this far.

The ridgelines meet overhead now, forming a natural arch. Curious. And wonderful! For the first time in thousands of hours, the planet Nep is completely hidden from his view. A verifiable change of scenery. Double darkness. It is like descending into a well, or a cavern.

Again he thinks of the song. About reading. And robbers.

The "cavern" narrows even more. Tiny lasers touch the walls, assuring XV that he is all right. He won't get stuck. Won't be impeded in any way. The road is clear. Still wide enough.

Onward. Processing. Checking. Looking. Searching. His visible eyes hoping for something aside from darkness. His rational heuristics comfortable either way.

He detects a variation in the light level. Barely perceptible, but his sensors assure him it is there. A less dim darkness. A greying from black. He pauses for a moment, checks the walls on both sides, then moves forward again.

Proteus is a silent world, without atmosphere, but if it were not so, the sound his treads make would change from crunching to a soft whirring. The surface of the ground is different. He also detects a curve in the tunnel. Makes the proper adjustment.

Then brightness reigns. He dials back his visual sensors. Wishes for arms to shield his face. Turns his head regardless.

He has entered a place unexpected.

For here, there is light.

The walls of the chamber are shades of brown and gold, and there is a certifiable symmetry to the patterns. A framework of narrow arches that loop all the way around. The chamber is barely larger than XV himself. Five-point-seven meters, his instruments tell him. The ceiling above is just over half that distance.

In the exact center of the chamber is an object. A bump. A mound? It is perfectly symmetrical. In appearance it is like four meter-wide balls arranged in the form of a pyramid. So, from most angles, one ball atop two, though it is really one ball atop three.

They are all shining brilliantly. Spectacularly. Generating light out of the darkness.

Tentatively, XV extends his heat-sensing device, moves it carefully toward the object. It registers no temperature change whatsoever. The mound is generating light, but no heat. Remarkable.

He performs a battery of tests: spectral analysis, air sample, wind speed. Nothing unusual. The chamber might as well be out on the surface. It is all normal. Proteus normal.

Except it isn't. Not at all.

His presumption of volcanic action is dismissed. As is the effect of hydraulics or pneumatics. Neither fire, nor water, nor air formed this place. Arranged the pyramid of shining balls.

Then what?

He contemplates the harvesters. They are the only creatures on the moon that can transport substance, aside from him. They have limited intelligence, however. They would see no reason to make such a place. They would allocate no time for such an endeavor. They have one solitary purpose: harvest the graxin he finds. Contain it, strip it, grind it, and extract it. That is what harvesters do. Quickly and efficiently. Like metal locusts.

So what causes this? Why is it here?

XV shakes his head. He has no idea. No human has ever been here. Aerial surveys were done. Graxin was found. He was deployed. Thousands of hours ago.

He thinks of planet Nep. That world is a sea of chilled gas. Crushing forces. Hydrogen, helium and "ices" such as methane and ammonia. Not the most adverse place in the solar system, but very nearly so.

Yet this chamber exists. Here. It is wonderful. Surprising. Unusual.

And constructed. Has to be.

Hidden. Out of sight.

His song speaks of flashlights. Shining!

This is all outside his experience. Beyond his programming. No rules govern this. There aren't even suggestions.

XV swivels his head to look at the tunnel behind him. He should go. Return to his perpetual mission. Processing. Sampling. Searching. Leave this place for whatever specter had built it.

He looks at the mound again. Does it have a purpose? Did it ever? He can make no guesses. He doesn't have the context to guess. To theorize. Not about this. It is wonderful, though. A welcome diversion. An anomaly.

His chronometer chimes. He has been in this chamber too long. Over an hour. Made no contact to the home, to the harvesters that wait. They will worry. Come to find him.

He reverses his motivator. Starts to back up the hall. Eyes fixed on the chamber of light. The brilliance of it. Rainbows seem to dance.

A question stops him. He draws carefully back into the chamber. What brought him here? Bots know nothing of chance. Of destiny.

Only one reason could be possible. Reluctantly, XV extends his most important sensor. Digs deeply into the floor of the chamber. Samples. Retracts the sensor slowly. Almost reverentially. Pulverizes the sample, sifts it...tastes it.

His motivator quickens. The chamber floor is nearly 90 percent graxin. He suspects the same could be said of the entire chamber. Those arches...the color is right. It is a veritable hoard. A lifetime of searching, combined into a single six-meter area.

His decision matrix shifts. Thought granules move, churn, spin, and plateau.

What should he do? The normal pathway is short. Simple. Signal home, bring the locusts.

His ever-smiling face pivots, turns, examines the chamber both up and down. Then he looks to the ground. Shakes his head.

Postponement. He is allowed that. Decisions can be belayed. Especially when safety is a concern.

The harvesters will wonder about his safety. He retreats. Makes his way out.

Hurrying.

XV reaches the place where the ridge above begins to separate and feels the blue-green glow of Nep overhead. Specifically, he notices the curl of the planet's Great Dark Spot. A storm that has been raging for millennia. A storm that is constant. Consistent. Violent.

He scans the horizon around him. Notes the grey and slate palette. Also consistent. Constant. Placid.

Yet he finds that his system is galvanized. His fluid flow rate is excessive given the situation. He authorizes correction routines, then runs a system diagnostic. Demands a slowdown. He still finds himself searching the surroundings. Digitally nervous.

There is no one here. Nothing to fear.

He redirects his thoughts. Forces his mind through familiar channels. Processing. Scanning. Always looking for more. Completing his mission. Finding graxin.

Humming. He needs to hum.

No bunnies, no kittens, no parrots.

The melody helps, but it doesn't restore his processes. Not completely. Something new has entered the matrix. Something he'll have to deal with.

No!

He deliberately moves ahead. Recalls normality. All he need do is find more graxin. Call the harvesters again.

He urges his treads to speed. Yes. He will find more graxin.

But not here. Nowhere close to here.

An hour later, XV locates the substance beneath a large and solitary outcropping of stone. His systems immediately relax. His decision matrix is satisfied. Temporarily.

He makes the call to the harvesters, but this time he waits for their arrival.

They bounce in on what appears to him to be legs made of nothing. Veritable whips beneath their shining round bodies. With only a passing acknowledgement of his presence, they begin to burrow and dance. First five harvesters arrive, and then a dozen. They circle the area, picking it clean of all the precious material they can find. Moving like silver piranhas amidst a sea of charcoal. Little furrows in the sand. Digging and consuming, leaping into the sky before they reach another location. Tenacious grazing.

They have graxin sensors of their own, of course. Short-range sensors.

Nothing as sophisticated as those in XV's array of instruments. Thankfully.

XV shakes his head. Checks the blue-green planet again. He gets a power low reminder then. It is time for him to return home.

He watches as the harvesters reach the end of their task. Begin bouncing and skipping away toward the horizon. He follows them. Slowly. Every sensor turned inward to conserve.

Two hours later he reaches the white silo he calls home. Noting his arrival, the curved door slides aside, allowing him entry. It has an external manual lock. He has no idea why. It is vestigial. Another leftover mystery. Human mystery.

XV turns, reverses himself into the entrance. Aligns himself over the sunken charging station. He then feels the pressure of the cable as it ascends from beneath. The prick as the spigot attaches to his undercarriage. Feels the energy begin to flow. A burning wholeness.

Home is as utilitarian within as it appears from without. Only the necessary equipment amidst a room of antiseptic white. White walls, with grey mechanical arms on each side to break up the monotony. The required repair and refueling equipment. Little else.

White ceiling.

While he waits, XV attempts to tabulate his finds of the day. His successes. He cannot exclude the chamber, however. Can't block it out.

What makes it important? Special? Why is it any different than the kilometers of gravel and dirt he travels every day?

He does not know, but it is special. And not because of the large quantity of graxin.

Light in the darkness. Something that should not be. Something unusual.

It includes a large amount of the substance he seeks. It should be completely harvested. It is why he is here. On Proteus.

The decision matrix stalls. Flips twice. Granules move in the opposite direction.

He can't make that call. Can't harvest it.

So, should he just ignore it? Act as if the chamber was never found? Yes. That is what he'll do.

XV deactivates his visual sensors—his eyes—and puts himself on half power. Now he will rest.

The decision is made.

Except the decision is not made. The very next day, XV finds himself again at the chamber. He searched for hours trying to avoid it, yet here he is, inside. Again.

Directly before him is the mound. The light is not constant, he realizes. Aside from the rainbows, there is a slight fluctuation in the light source. A feeling of life. Of permanence.

More curious now, he brings additional sensors to bear. He reaches out and samples the walls. He is surprised to find the remnants of a color additive laid atop the wall's surface. Designs had been painted there. He examines their structure across the spectrum. Yes, there are telltale coloring changes. A pattern. Drawings of bipeds. It might even be a story.

He references the few human records he has. Trying to find a starting point, a similarity between what was and what he sees. But sadly, he has very little to work with. Luxuries like history, philosophy, and theology aren't necessary for a sampling bot. Especially one so far from the blue dot. Way out here.

His systems grieve for his lack. His disability. His creators gave him the capacity to hum and wonder—along with a painted smile—but nothing of real value. Nothing of depth. Only a task. An existence wholly defined by what he does.

He searches the room again. Wishes for the ability to really smile.

He has this now, though. A special place.

He nods. Yes. He has this.

Hundreds of hours go by. Hours of graxin searching mingled with visits to the chamber. No longer does he try to measure or probe its mysteries. All he does is sit and marvel. Delight in the colors. In the shimmering light.

Irreducible glory.

He derives theories as to its origin. To its purpose. That perhaps Proteus once was populated, or that it was visited by extra-solar people. Travelers.

It is a captured moon, he knows. One that could have come from farther out. Out where the ice dwarfs live. Perhaps beyond Pluto and Eris and Haumea. Out where no probe or bot has ever been. No eye has ever seen.

Or maybe, just maybe, the chamber was formed with the moon. Made especially for him...

It is all wild speculation. Yet he revels in it anyway. It makes the rest of his chores seem easier. Less mundane.

But still trivial in comparison.

It is during his most speculative and fulfilling visit that he ignores his chronometer. Forgets the time. Loses his place. Loses track.

And things change.

He exits the tunnel, backing out as he always does. He isn't two meters from the exit before his rear sensors detect something. Movement. A tingle of energy, nervousness, travels his pathways. He pivots and swings his body around. Aims the triangle pilot away from the entrance.

And he sees it.

Sitting completely still on the ground. Watching. Whip-like legs totally at rest, hanging like strands of hair from its side.

A single harvester. Shiny, silver, lone aperture for an eye. Nothing but blackness beyond that. Behind it. And it watches XV, having just exited the tunnel.

At first XV thinks the harvester is incapacitated, it remains so still. But the use of a radiation sensor tells him the harvester is functioning. It is alive.

Perhaps it is damaged? He sends a message to the silver spider, asking for its ident. After a short pause, it answers. The parity checks are correct. The harvester is fine. Only temporarily immobile. Voluntarily watching.

XV asks an important question: "Why are you here?"

The harvester studies him. XV can feel the tickle of its rudimentary sensors in action. Probing him. Looking for anomalies. Finally, the probing stops. "Your extended absence was detected. I was sent to find you. Determine if you need assistance. Do you?"

"I do not," XV messages back. "I am fully operational. Here's my latest system diagnostic and comparative baseline spec." He sends the data along. Waits.

Finally, the harvester moves. Sits up on its arms. Straightens. It then turns slightly, as if peering behind XV. "Were you encumbered?" Meaning "delayed due to situational circumstances."

XV bows his head. "I was. A narrow passage. Requiring slow movement."

"Is this place useful for harvesting? Should others come?"

XV feels the granules of his matrix begin to flutter and take flight. They spin around his cranium like a small sandstorm. Choking his reaction. Clogging the pathways. How should he answer?

"No fish!" says the song. Fish don't walk.

He shakes his head slowly.

With a slight nod, the harvester turns and bounces away.

XV pauses for a long moment. Scans the dark horizon, and then the giant overhead. He must return to work.

He can't ignore the disjointed thoughts that interfere. The fact that he doesn't want to leave.

Concern fills him. Worry that his chamber has now been discovered. What if the harvester doesn't believe him? What if some anomaly showed up in its scans? What if it returns with the rest? The swirling, burrowing, unthinking rest.

The chamber would be destroyed. Completely.

He reassesses his thought processes. Bids the granules to slow, settle.

The harvester suspected nothing. It won't be back. XV will move on.

He waits another five minutes, just to be certain. Checks the surroundings again with all available sensors. Detects nothing. No motion whatsoever.

He resumes his work.

For hundreds of hours he avoids the chamber completely. He never waits for the harvesters to do their work. He simply calls them and moves on to the next find.

He even returns home for another charge. Yet while he is recharging, he is certain he hears the harvesters in the building plotting. Asking questions behind his back. Wondering about the exquisite find he is withholding. Hoarding. Questioning his sanity. His purpose.

Finally, he is certain what he must do. He'll never beat the harvesters in raw speed. They are too agile, too quick. So after his charge is complete, he leaves the white silo behind. He travels the now familiar path all the way to the place where the parallel ridges begin to converge. He doesn't bother to enter the chamber again. He knows what that will bring. The time it will require.

Instead, he turns and backs himself in as tight as possible. Fills the chamber's entrance with his bulk.

Then he waits.

Eventually, they come.

There are ten of them this time. They travel in the normal way, skipping and bouncing. There is no indication that this time is any different. No reverence for where they now are. They simply form a semi-circle two meters before him. And stop. Look at him.

"Why are you at this location again?" one of them messages.

XV holds his place. "I prefer it."

This brings more silence.

"Prefer?" The group turns toward each other. "No failures are sensed in this model. Yet its messages make no sense."

"We message over the same frequency," XV says, reminding them that he is present.

The harvesters appraise him again. "Tell us your purpose here. Is there graxin?"

XV readies his sensing devices. Steels himself. "It doesn't matter," he messages back.

The harvesters stall for a moment. "Doesn't matter? That is an inconsistent answer."

One harvester breaks free from the group. It begins slowly walking, like a silver daddy longlegs, to the perimeter of the clearing. It turns toward the ground, sniffing, scanning. It then stops and begins to bounce. "Graxin detected!"

The others leave formation and begin to circle the area. They get more agitated as they move. Some begin to harvest right there, others merely circle, as if unsure where to start. One—with the call letters HV-21—follows the ground unceasingly until it collides with XV's triangular pilot. His pushing structure. "The readings get stronger this way," it says. "There must be more. Behind." It appraises XV with its single black eye. "Please reposition, XV."

He shakes his ever-smiling head. "I will not."

The harvesters cease their churning. They quickly regroup in front of him. Close up. "You must move," they say in unison. "We cannot perform our task."

He shakes his head. "I will not."

The harvesters break into a frenzy, circling like ants caught in a thunderstorm. "You must," they repeat over and over, messages buzzing like mosquitoes in his receptors. "You must!"

But he does not.

Then the harvesters begin to leap. Trying to go over him. Around him.

He extends all his sensors. Engages everything that can do damage. Anything that has weight or heat. He moves and swivels. Pushes.

Arms sprawl. The battle is joined. XV begins to hum.

Love needs something to protect. Scare away the dark.

It is six thousand hours before the ship from the blue dot arrives. The human passengers find XV parked alone within the silo. Home. His systems are in hibernate mode, the proper disposition for a bot in the process of charging.

Solstice, the younger of the two astronauts, walks to one of the interior walls and begins checking gauges. "There's a fair amount of graxin here," he says, squinting through his suit visor. "Can't seem to find any of the harvesters, though. There should be harvesters around, right? Cloistered above?"

Longstring, ever the weathered commander, shakes his head. "Probably out on a find." He indicates the sleeping XV. "These things keep them busy. Always searching. Sniffing it out." He nods toward a mounted screen. "Check the local stream."

XV awakens from his sleep. Moves smoothly forward.

The astronauts both pause, watching as he moves toward the open door.

"See there," Longstring says finally. "Busy."

Solstice shrugs and sidesteps left. Peers closely at the screen. "No idents whatsoever." A puzzled look. "What does that mean?"

XV exits the silo, waits outside. The door begins to close.

Longstring joins Solstice at the gauges. Shakes his head. "It means we should go and look. We'll need to get some long-range scanning equipment. Have to be thorough."

XV begins to hum.

How much is that doggie in the window?

"Fine with me," Solstice says. "A little excitement. Up for some exploring when we're through? They say Proteus is one of the darkest places in the system. A captured moon. Never know what you may find..."

The silo door closes completely. XV unfolds a sensor arm. Uses it to manipulate the external manual lock. He then turns, begins his journey.

Processing, always processing. Finding the indicators. Gathering data. Deciding. Marking or discarding. Perpetually at work. Performing his mission. His new mission.

Behind him, he hears pounding on the door. Pleas to return. To set them free. Limited time. Limited air!

His painted face only looks ahead. Toward his chamber. His purpose.

Humans would only strip it down.

THREADBARE

My whole world is this green-painted garage. Heavy grease lines the walls, the paint is chipped in multiple places. There are stacks of tools and bot parts lying around. Greasy, grimy mounds. I'm as afraid of falling as I am of infection.

It's been an hour since my last job, and I'm nervous. "A debugger that isn't moving is dying." Lots of truth to that. I run a greasy hand over my bald head, anxious for one of the heavies to come in before I'm deemed unnecessary. Usually fixing heavies is good. Sometimes they explode on you, though—not so good.

I hear the clank-clank of the garage door, and it begins to slide open. Okay, not as nervous now. Something is coming.

The machine rolls in, and it looks flawless, painted tan and brown. Hardly a nick on it. The head is large and solid, slightly conical. It blends into the shoulders with little in the way of a neck. Powerful arms, able to extend, full of armaments. Bone-crushing treads. Perfect for defending against the Imam's enemies.

The implant in my head receives a message. I close my eyes to read it. Bot performs inadequately in battle.

Not much to go on, but I power the bot down and look everything over. The weapons all work, the brain seems to have the right code. Numbers all check out. Treads operate—I even power it on and make it do a figure eight around the greasy, grimy mounds. Nothing unusual there.

Finally, I bring out a diagnostic sheet and smooth it over the bot's cranium. The surface becomes transparent, allowing me to look inside. Nanopaths and conduits. A rainbow of color. One would think that models like this would have simple designs: See enemy, kill enemy! But in actuality, they're the most complicated. Especially their decision matrices. Like bees in a honeycomb.

Plus, they sometimes overload and the bot explodes.

After staring inside for an hour, I find nothing. There's some randomness built into these heavy personalities, though. Otherwise they do crazy things like get themselves stuck while following orders. I'm guessing the problem is in the randomness.

I sigh and slap the thing on its head. "Rails, what's wrong with you?" Probably not my smartest move, the head-slapping. Explosives and all.

"MS-77 is ready." Its voice shakes my implant, nearly breaking my drums.

"Volume down," I say. "Can you help me, please?"

"My orders are—"

I laugh. "Yeah, orders. Why don't you fight? You're programmed to."

"There is a logic inconsistency."

I use my implant to digitally touch the bot's matrix. Much of its design is a mystery, but I do some compares with known specs. There are places here that might be inconsistent. I knead the matrix code. Hope for the best.

"How are you now?" I ask. "Ready to smash some infidels?"

The bot looks at me. "I must not harm a human being."

"What?"

"Harming one of A's creations is forbidden. Battle may—"

"Great! I've flipped a heavy into a pacifist!"

"What is your request?"

"A list too long to stream. Let me try a few more things…" I try hours of things. I even attempt to back out everything I've done. The heavy remains aggressively neutral.

"Where did this altruism come from?" Bots have rules, but in one of these hulks, preservation of life should be far down the list.

"You're my most recent DR," it says. "Any responsibility—"

"Oh no. Don't go blaming this on me. You were broken when you got here."

"My current configuration came from DR-23, moniker ThreadBare. You are—?"

"I am," I sigh. Sometimes these low-flow bots attach like baby ducks. Comes in handy in battle. Not so much here. "Fine. I command you to accept this change to your matrix: Do not value human—" I stop myself. I'm in a locked garage with a killing machine. Nuance, Thread. Use it.

I clear a spot on the nearest counter and sit down. Stare at the bot. It stares at me. We sit that way a long time.

"Fighting for your country should be in there," I say. "Way up there."

"Insufficient weight. Logic problem remains."

Rails, this guy is tough. I think hard, then snap my fingers. "You value human life, right?"

"I must not harm—"

"Sure. But what if by not acting you cause harm? That wouldn't be good either, right?"

The bot goes silent, then begins to rock on its treads. I swear I see smoke coming from its ports. "Logic inconsistency. Matrix fault eminent. Involuntary weapon discharge—"

"Wait! Don't do that, you'll hurt me! Me, ThreadBare. Sitting right here."

The smoke diminishes. The rocking stops. "Must not harm human being. Must not hurt DR-23."

"Right, that's right. Settle, big fellow." I have an idea. "MS-77, what if you use my safety as a guide?"

The bot stares at me.

"Instead of the general, focus on the specific. Protect one human."

The bot's head rotates forward. There's a long silence, and I expect smoke again. Or a big boom. Finally, it looks at me. "Inconsistency nullified. I will do it for you, DR-23."

"Fine. Fight for me, ya brute."

I check its matrix another time. It doesn't lie. All appears placid. Really smooth. I wave the bot away. "Back to battle, you." It watches me all the way out.

I act like I don't care. But it still bothers me. Someone fighting for me.

Six days later, I catch a news report. This one sticks because it's about a heavy that was destroyed in battle, smashed beyond repair. It was out of position, away from its battle group. Acting erratically, before it drove into the path of an enemy rocket.

The rocket was headed toward the city. Left unchecked, it would've hit a school.

A special school. One for debuggers like me.

I don't know that it was MS-77. The report doesn't say.

But I like to think it was.

SECRETS

The secrets found me, I swear.

It was only my second month at the corporation. I was hired as an actuary right from the university. My desk was one of hundreds of desks in this giant cavern of a place. It was claustrophobic, despite the size. I did like the colors, though. A mixture of deep reds and purples. It made me feel almost regal. Important.

I was one of so many, though. All of us staring, trance-like, at our personal projected light screens. Moving numbers in space. A naïve observer would think us mental patients, the hundreds of us waving our hands and fluttering our eyes. Or possibly that we were members of a galactic symphony, missing only a conductor. Directing ourselves.

It started with my break time. I swiped off my screen, stood, and without looking at the others, made my way to the door. Even the door felt fancy, it had the appearance of real wood, thickly varnished.

There was a security officer stationed next to it, a sleek weapon strapped to his side. He acknowledged my presence with a nod. "You have thirty minutes, Actuary Renise Bryant."

I smiled and returned the nod. It was the same thing he always said. So personable.

I took a step forward, heard a soft click, and the door slid open.

The hallway beyond was more austere then my "office," but still polished. Dark paneling and noise-dampening carpet, pictures of company accomplishments lined the walls. Models we'd constructed and delivered. Advanced designs of war and flight.

I moved quietly and with purpose as all young actuaries are instructed. Ahead was an intersection from which five hallways split off. Instinctively I smoothed my hair, then my blouse and pants. I never knew who I might meet.

As I reached the intersection, someone exited the hall to my left. It was a Terran male, slight in build, with seemingly perfect, dark hair. He was properly dressed, but his clothing was a size too large. A bit droopy. Adjunct Jadder Franks.

Jadder smiled when he saw me. "Miss Bryant—well, hello."

I smiled politely. "Mister Franks." I took a step toward the rightmost hallway, the one that led to the lavatory. Adjuncts are behavior experts. They help with marketing and sales, so consequently, they exude personality. I could never do his job, and I was leery of those that did.

"You seem a bit distracted there," he said. "On your break?"

"Yes, I have—"

"Things are wonderful in M and S, by the way. Lots of beautiful products coming." He spread his fingers. "Lots of intergalactic buzz." He swooped closer. "I'd love to show it all to you. It is larger than space. Bigger than a foldgate."

I took another step toward my goal. Another step away.

"Of course, I couldn't because of clearance..." He closed the gap. "Your department is incredible too, obviously. Lot going on there, I've heard. Important calculations."

My department was neither incredible nor important. It was simply necessary. None of us really knew what we were working on. Not the whole picture. We only moved numbers endlessly.

"Yes..." I glanced down the hallway again. "Um...I need to—"

Jadder snapped his fingers. "Ah yes, limited break time. I know, I know. They tried that in the ole M and S once." He smiled brightly. "Didn't go so well." He pointed down the hall. "I'll walk with you so we can talk."

I nodded, but I wanted to be free. For the next five minutes I learned about Jadder's personal vehicle, his last off world excursion, and the time he saw his first cyber relic. It was a fascinating conversation. For him.

It wasn't the first time I'd been so encumbered either, but Jadder seemingly didn't remember.

When we arrived at the row of lavatory doors, I approached the one designated "Terran Female" and hesitated. "Well, this is me..." I expected him to go about his business. But he didn't. He lingered instead, studying me.

I raised a hand.

He subtly rocked on his heels, still smiling. "Oh, I can wait," he said. "I have plenty of time."

I shook my head. "I might be awhile." I tried to be perky. "You know us women!"

He waved a hand dismissively. "No problem whatsoever. We're used to waiting in M and S. All planning and waiting."

I forced a giggle. "Well, you should get back to your planning then. I'm sure you'll be missed. You're important."

"Thank you, yes, but..." He glanced at the door three over from mine. "I suppose I could use the facilities myself while I'm here. Then we can talk more."

I suppressed a groan, nodded, and touched the lavatory door, causing it to open.

The room was fragranced with a subtle spice scent. That helped a little.

After the door closed, I stepped to the reflective wall next to it. I checked that my hair was straight and that my shoes still retained their luster. Then I counted to ten and touched the door again. It slid aside and I peeked out.

No Jadder.

I quietly stepped into the hall, turned left, and did my best to tiptoe away. There had to be another lavatory on the floor somewhere. I reached the next corner in about twelve steps, and ducking around it, quickened my pace.

Away.

The further I walked, the more enamored I became with the facility. I had limited time, sure, but even the security guard would understand wanting to avoid Jadder.

Each room was immaculately decorated. Even the hallways were interesting, with much to delight the senses. They spoke of the wealth of the company, its near-permanence, and its attention to detail.

Why hadn't they shown me all this during orientation?

I knew why, of course. Actuaries were deliberately kept focused—and focus meant limited distractions. I checked my timecom device to be certain I was still all right. I had twenty minutes left.

I continued to wander, but with purpose. I reached a room filled with green floor covering and rows of glass shelving. The shelves had miniature displays of more company designs—everything from battle suits to star carriers. Many of the designs had embossed awards projected over them. I paused beside a model that represented a particularly agile battle suit. I squinted at the label. Pilot design, Waylox Design Team.

Wonderful!

I heard Jadder's voice, and my heart skipped. It sounded like he was approaching behind me, generally in the way I'd come. There were two other routes out of the room. One was to my left and a fair distance away. The other was ahead past more shelving, but it appeared to have a silver pass restriction. My pass was only grey.

I heard Jadder's voice again. I frowned, and scanning the room, noticed an interior corner. I quickly stepped around it.

Jadder entered with another Terran female in tow.

Already?

Her less formal apparel proved she wasn't from my department. The doll eyes she was giving Jadder suggested she wasn't from *his* department either. I doubted anyone could spend much time with him and still be enamored. But Jadder was prattling along as usual, and she seemed delighted to listen.

Maybe she thinks it will get her somewhere? Move her up the ladder?

I shook my head. Couldn't see it.

They approached the secured door, and Jadder waved his hand in front of it. It clicked and slid aside.

I couldn't help but notice the hallway beyond. It featured large holographic images—possibly the newer designs Jadder had mentioned. The "larger than space" stuff. I wanted to examine them, if only to say that I had.

Jadder and the other woman walked through, still talking. She apparently had silver clearance. Or Jadder was bending the rules for her.

Figures.

I stepped around the corner just as the security door began to close. I frowned as the hallway beyond—those curious new designs—started to disappear from sight. I heard Jadder's voice soften as he and his companion walked away.

The door closed but then reopened slightly. I watched it for a few moments, expecting Jadder or someone else to come walking through. But no one did.

A wave glitch? I'd heard of such things. Strange that in a company steeped in technology that sometimes the doors misfire. But they do. This time they did.

I walked toward the door, forgetting my time limit and the risk. I paused at the threshold, and leaned in to see if anyone was watching the door, Jadder especially. The hallways beyond, of which there were three, looked empty.

I stepped through.

I expected to be stopped shortly thereafter, told that I was beyond my clearance, and then sent, roughly, back to Actuary. I maintained my purposeful stride, though, hoping that it would indicate I belonged there to whoever monitored security.

I knew I couldn't take much time. I had to quickly sate my desire and get back. My whole spine was tingling.

The hallways here were decidedly larger, allowing for life-size holograms. I approached the first display. It featured a more formidable creation than the pilot suit I'd seen in the outer room. This one towered over me, and while it approximated the human form, there were large conduits wrapped around it that gave it an alien appearance—as if an octopus rode a human's back. It looked both cruel and irresistible. There was an impressive weapon in the hologram's hands as well. A rifle larger than my leg.

I glanced at the security door again and frowned. I should be getting back to work, but instead I drifted to the next display, and the next.

A few minutes later, I was startled by footsteps. My instincts yelled "Security!" and my pulse began to race. The door I'd entered through was a fair distance away. Running would only create a lot of racket. And make me look guilty.

There was another door nearby, so I quickly moved to that one and touched the surface. It didn't budge. I cursed softly and checked for another escape route.

I spotted a door across the hall and scurried to it. That one opened to my touch, so I darted inside and willed the door to close. Shortly before it finished, a large group of people walked by.

I held my breath, waiting for the crowd to leave the area. Then I chuckled at my newfound bravado. My recklessness. I checked the time again: only ten minutes left.

I heard voices behind me. I spun around, terrified.

I saw rows of blue audio cubicles, each with their own chair and desk. I was in a small auxiliary conference room. A spillover facility used to house non-essential employees during departmental meetings. The kind of place I typically ended up in.

All the cubicles appeared empty, though. "Hello?" I said and slowly walked the length of the room.

I found no one.

I allowed myself a smile. One of the cubes must've been left on. That would explain the voices.

I moved through the cubes again, looking for the culprit.

I recognized the voice. It was the company's current CEO, Standon Rez. His tone wasn't as jovial as it was during company meetings, though. It was more reserved. Drained of its energy.

I found the active cube and took a seat within. The desk had audio and visual controls, but I was afraid to touch them. I didn't want to lose the sound. The CEO was talking numbers, and I was a sucker for numbers.

"We continue to be on target with actuary projections—"

Actuary?

"And deliveries?" It was a female voice, probably Terran. Strident and harsh.

"Deliveries to all interested parties proceed as expected," Rez said, "given the aforementioned shortages. If we could—"

There was a rumbling gasp, part brass instrument, part drowning man. "Pressure must be placed on them," a male voice echoed. Mechanical, thunderous, and frightening.

"We've taken the usual steps to bring the suppliers back in line. They promise—"

Another rumble, though this one seemed infused with amusement. "Contracts, promises, the corporation is beyond all that now. Pressure, Rez. Metal-fisted pressure."

"Brother..." The female again.

"The plan!" thunder voice said. "All bows to the plan."

"Yes, but one shouldn't cut off one's legs." The female paused, then chuckled. "An unfortunate choice of words. My apologies."

Next came a gargling sound. I didn't know what it signified, but it wasn't pleasant.

"Perhaps he's correct, Mr. Rez," the female said. "Numbers don't lie. Any delay could be disastrous. Thousands of years lost."

Thousands?

"I'll see what I can do," Mr. Rez said. "Exert pressure, as you say."

"As if your life depends on it," thunder voice said. "Because it does."

"*All* life does," the female said.

I glanced at my timecom. I needed to leave, but found I couldn't. I wanted to hear the "plan" that was mentioned.

And who were the people with Rez? Investors, or someone else?

Rez mentioned cybers. There were place names I didn't recognize and details I didn't understand. Then my department was highlighted along with obscure procedures and models. The references were enough that, whatever the plan was, the answer might be back there. In Actuary.

I needed to return, now more than ever. I shut down the cube, stood, and hurried back.

The guard gave me a long stare when I entered. I cemented my composure as best I could, keeping my back rigid and my tone even.

"Precisely thirty minutes, Actuary Renise Bryant," he said. "No more and no less."

I nodded, wishing I had another chance at the lavatory mirror. Did I look like I'd run back? Was my hair straight?

"Someone stole my lunch," I said. "I didn't have credits for another. I needed to find someone to..."

The guard continued to stare. A trickle of sweat ran down my back.

Finally, he nodded. "Your tardiness is noted, but excused." He leaned closer. "This time."

I flashed a smile and returned to my desk. I activated my screen and got to work, filling the air with motion. I shifted numbers in all directions. Playing the song I was hired to play.

But curiosity filled me. Every so often, every ten minutes or so, I shifted the numbers in an atypical way. I searched their waveforms, moved their tides and currents, and manipulated them in a direction to reveal hints of what I'd heard from Mr. Rez's presentation.

As the hours passed, I saw glimpses of what this "plan" might be.

The implications shocked me.

I could barely focus when I returned home that evening. Nothing on the entertainment channels interested me. Neither did the news or the other promptings the apartment gave me—hobbies I'd neglected, bills that needed payment, friends and family I hadn't spoken with in a while.

My close friend, Salento, contacted me on the central apartment com, but I feigned fatigue. Told her I'd call her in the morning.

I wasn't tired in any way, though. I was invigorated and disturbed. I knew a secret that was as massive as the galaxy. As cold as a rhat emperor's heart.

But what could I do about it?

My apartment had a half-circle design, with the central com as the focal point. I took a seat on the curved sofa in front of the com and tried to decide what to do next.

I had an old friend who was a journalist—Randix. He lived off planet now I thought, but someone should know where he was. He worked for one of the large syndicates.

I contacted Salento on the central com again.

"I knew you weren't tired." Salento was dressed nicer than the last time I saw her, and her hair was heavily curled. "I'm going out. Wanna come?"

"No," I said. "I need to sleep. I only wanted to..." Glancing at the floor, I dug my feet into the heavy, blue carpet. "Do you remember Randix?"

She raised an eyebrow. "Randix the snoop? Randix the tattler?"

"Yeah, that one. He was a decent guy, right?"

"For a snoop, sure." She frowned and leaned closer. "Why?"

"You know where he lives now?"

She gave me a strange look. "Why?"

I shrugged. "I need some text manipulated for work. A tattler would be a good resource, I think."

She shook her head. "Renise is going all nostalgic on me. Searching for past loves."

I slid into my Actuary demeanor. "Me? No. I have work—"

She chuckled. "Are you sure you don't want to come out?"

I made a show of removing my shoes and loosening the neck of my blouse. "Can't tonight, Sal. But soon, I promise."

My palms were sweating. I hadn't eaten all day. I should be hungry, but even now that urge was absent.

She studied me for a moment. "Randix, huh?"

"Yeah, I could really use his skills."

She sighed. "You're cutting into my fun time here, but I suppose I can help. If he spaced away somewhere, though, a message will take a long time. Almost better to visit."

I shrugged. "Could you at least check?"

She rolled her eyes. Patted at her hair. "Give me a minute." She ended the conversation.

While I waited, I found a travel sack and started to pack. It was the only thing I could think to do. I'd never been off world before, but this seemed like a special situation.

I threw in some clothing and some toiletries. Another handheld com device and as many free credits as I could find.

I recalled another company product I owned. A small handheld weapon. Would I need that? I found the dark pistol and tucked it into the sack's outside pocket.

The com chimed, and with a touch, Salento's image returned. I slid the sack onto the floor, out of sight, and took a seat in front of her.

"I think it's a lost cause, Renise. He's on Galite. It'll take days for a response. Maybe someone local can help?"

I shrugged. "Yeah, probably. Can you give me his specifics anyway?"

She nodded. "I'll send you Randix's location info. Everything I have. But he's far away. Too far to date."

The central com indicated receipt of Randix's information. I waved my handheld com near it which swallowed the data for later use.

"I'm going now, Renise," Salento said, feigning a pout. "I'll miss you."

"I'll miss you too." I returned her pouting face, then ended the conversation.

I made a last check of my bag, then scanned the room for anything else I might need. The quickest way to Galite would be to charter a ride. A charter was expensive, but worth it in this case.

Was I really doing this? Spacing to another world to search for someone I hadn't seen in years?

I remembered the secret, and the thundering voice I'd heard. It felt like I might know more than one secret. Like it might not only be the message but the messenger, as well.

Yes, I was going. Now, while someone could still stop it. Or at least make sense of it all.

An investigative "tattler" could do that. He could sift the facts and help me figure out what I'd heard. I nodded resolutely, hefted the pack, and turned for the door.

The door chimed.

I frowned and shook my head. Who was it? It was too late for guests.

I placed my bag near the entrance and leaned close. The door recognized my motion and its surface became transparent. On the other side was Jadder.

What was he doing here? Of all people! And how did he know where I lived?

We did have mutual acquaintances, of course. Friends that might share information to nurture any romantic tendencies.

I hated that. Especially when it brought Jadder to my door! I could've not answered, but Jadder had already proven himself persistent. He might wait outside all night.

I checked my appearance and touched the door.

As soon as it opened, Jaddar rushed forward and attempted to grab my neck. I managed to duck his hands, but he still barreled into me, knocking us both to the floor.

I rolled away from him "Jadder! What are you—?"

He scrambled toward me, and got ahold of my left foot. I kicked at him with my other foot while trying to move toward the door. Toward escape.

"Snooping around where you don't belong, huh?" he gasped.

I dug into the carpeting and attempted to pull myself free. Jadder was stronger than he looked. "What?"

"Found something interesting," he said. "Something outside your department."

I kicked hard and managed to free my foot. "I don't know what you're talking about!" I said. "You're crazy!" I tried to stand, but he pulled me down again. My shoulder impacted hard on something, causing my right arm to go numb. The door was a meter away. If only I could—

He started to crawl his way up my body. I was repulsed by every touch. I beat on his head, then I grabbed his perfect hair and pulled.

He yelled and swore at me. "I have another job," he said. "Another group that's really going places. Silent Company, have you heard of them?"

"No!" I said. "Now, get off!"

He cackled. "The reason you haven't heard of us is because no one speaks after we've found them." He pulled his face closer. "That's why it's silent, get it? We're silent because we do the silencing."

"Clever." I pushed on his face with my left hand. Dug in with my nails. More grunts and curses.

Feeling returned to my right arm, so I flung it toward the door. Grabbed the carpet again. Attempted to move.

"I have you, sorry," he said. "So sorry we never got more acquainted."

I shouted my disgust and reached again. My hand touched the travel sack. It was still open. I exploded with all my remaining energy. Struggling with everything I had. My fingers felt something hard inside the bag. My gun.

I managed to circle the hilt with my thumb and forefinger. Pulled it free.

Jadder hit my face hard. "No more of that," he said. "No screaming."

Pain blinded me. I couldn't see, but my arm stayed in motion. I brought the gun back to me. Pointed it. And fired.

There was a flash and a feeling of release. Secrets. Galite. Randix.

I would make it to Galite.

PROTEUS

Proteus's hue was an anomaly, a seeming mockery of its parent, Neptune. That planet—all science officer Jackal could see from his position in the flight deck of reconnaissance ship Jambiya—was solid blue. No pinks like its circling satellite. No browns or greens like Earth. Only blue.

"Why are we here again?" ship pilot Serif asked.

Jackal shot him a look. "You didn't forget. I don't—"

Serif waved him off. "Yeah. Accident inspection and ore recovery. I know." He pointed a thumb at the window. "It's oppressive, Neptune. Too large. Too blue."

"That isn't our worry. Only finding the lost ship and recovering its ore." Jackal squinted at his screen's topography of the moon. Proteus was an ugly place. Not large enough to have formed a perfect sphere, but almost. A skewed, heavily-cratered polyhedron. "Missed it by that much."

"Missed what?" Serif looked his way.

"Nothing." Jackal felt a tickle of apprehension. "Not seeing anything here. You?"

"Nope. No distress signals. No location pulses. Nothing." Serif touched a couple green spots on his screen's surface. "Where could it be?"

Jackal shook his head. "Nothing in the visual band either. Like it vanished."

"Exploded?"

"Should be a debris field, right? No sign of that." His screen highlighted various locations on the moon's surface. "There are metal markers, but Proteus has graxin reserves. Always messes with orbital scans."

"I have the ship's last known location."

"Good. Then that's where we should land."

Two hours later, they rested atop a generally level plain amidst a panorama of crags and mountains. Uncertain dangers. Proteus's pinkness was subtle here. Barely perceivable. Hidden.

Further scans showed little trace of the ship, or its crew, aside from a single, anomalous reading. They suited up to investigate using the ship's two-seated rover.

"Where to?" Serif said as they rumbled onto the surface.

Jackal studied the rover's scans. "Still showing non-ferrous metals to the west." He pointed left. "That way."

Serif gunned the engine and they were underway. They skirted massive craters and jutting hills. Neptune ruled the sky. Minutes passed.

Serif broke the silence. "There are mining bots here somewhere, right? Might be picking those up."

"Maybe. The largest is about the size of the rover. An XV unit. Four meters square, treaded. Has a collection basket in front, round head on top. Here, I'll show you." Jackal produced an image of the XV on his screen.

Serif studied the image, then pointed to the robot's head. "Is that a face on there?"

Jackal snorted. "Yeah, engineering does that sort of thing. Paints faces to make them seem human." He shook his head. "Silly."

Serif nodded. "What about the others?"

"Harvester drones. They're smaller." He brought up a drone image.

"Like fat spiders."

Jackal chuckled. "With an appetite for minerals scraped from crushed rocks."

"How do they do that?"

Jackal couldn't help himself. "Guess they have sharp teeth."

"Great." Serif looked toward the horizon. "I'll keep my eyes open."

Thirty minutes later, they reached the source of the readings. It was... unexpected.

A five-meter-high pyramid, as aesthetically imperfect as the moon it stood upon, and seemingly made from whatever materials were available. Poles jutted out at odd angles or stopped too soon. Metal plating and other flat items formed the outer surface.

Serif stopped the rover ten meters away. "Close enough? Don't want to mess with your analysis."

"It's fine," is all Jackal could manage. He got out and Serif followed. Jackal carried a handheld com unit, tied to the rover's scanning array. As they approached the structure, he studied its many intriguing and seemingly contradictory results. "The materials came from our lost ship. In fact, I think they were the ship." He indicated the pyramid's top. "Except whatever that is up there."

The pinnacle was composed of ten glowing spheres arranged in the shape of a smaller pyramid. Their precise chemical composition was hard to nail down. At times, they didn't even appear solid.

"Trans-dimensional?" Jackal muttered. "Possibly extrasolar."

"What?" Serif laid a gloved hand against the side of the pyramid. "Feels normal to me."

"No. The top. The shiny spheres."

Serif patted his helmet, then searched the horizon in all directions. "Who did it? Who built this?" He looked at Jackal. "The crewmembers? What were their names? Longstring and Solstice?"

"I don't..." Jackal noticed something on the structure and walked closer. The edges of every part, every post and plating, showed a similar swirled pattern of scrapes. "Look at these." He pointed. "That's not from being dragged over the surface. Looks more like machine handling." He examined a place where a plate attached to a support pole. "And how is this put together? Looks welded here, but up here..." He pointed at a higher spot. "It's glued." He stepped to the right, squatted. "And down here, bound together with string." His trepidation returned. "At least, I think that's string..."

"Using whatever they had. Reusing and repurposing."

Jackal's stomach lurched and he gasped for air. Sweat stung his eyes. "Whatever happened here wasn't good. And I think those spheres are the cause." He took a step toward the rover. "We need to get back. Report this."

His comm unit chirped, then the screen exploded with new readings. Metallic objects. Motion. He looked to the horizon and saw rolling, metal spheres. Harvesters. They encircled the men and the rover within seconds.

"Run!"

The XV robot—the one with the face—rolled into view. As the harvesters closed in, the XV trundled toward them, a mechanical arm raised.

Serif made a retching sound.

"Serif?"

Another cough. "We know where one of the men went, Jackal. Look at its face!"

The robot's head wore a mask now. The front of a skull. Glued into place.

"He got recycled!"

Jackal tore his vision away. Focused on the rover. On reaching safety.

A harvester smashed into him, pushing him to the ground. He realized then. In Neptune's shadow, Proteus wasn't pink at all.

It was red.

MORE WORLDS AWAIT...

That's all the dreams for now, but I have over a dozen novels.
Want another robot story like *Graxin* and *A Symphony of Words*?
Check out the just-released *Lost Bits*!

You can find *Lost Bits* on Amazon.

And if you haven't read my original cyberpunk trilogy yet, there's
no better time. The first book is free simply for signing up for my
newsletter list.

You can get *A Star Curiously Singing* at www.KerryNietz.com. Thanks
for reading!

YOU CAN MAKE A DIFFERENCE!

Word-of-mouth marketing is the best kind. Not only does it ensure that good books get noticed, it also helps bring the right books to the people who will enjoy them most.

If this story met or exceeded your expectations in any way, please consider telling your friends and/or posting a short review.

Your help is greatly appreciated!

ABOUT THE AUTHOR

Kerry Nietz is an award-winning science fiction author. He has over a dozen speculative novels in print, along with a novella, a couple short stories, and a nonfiction book, *FoxTales*.

Kerry's novel *A Star Curiously Singing* won the Readers Favorite Gold Medal Award for Christian Science Fiction and is notable for its dystopian, cyberpunk vibe in a world under sharia law. It is often mentioned on "Best of" lists.

Among his writings, Kerry's most talked about is the genre-bending *Amish Vampires in Space*. AViS was mentioned on the *Tonight Show* and in the *Washington Post, Library Journal,* and *Publishers Weekly*. *Newsweek* called it "a welcome departure from the typical Amish fare."

Kerry is a refugee of the software industry. He spent more than a decade of his life flipping bits, first as one of the principal developers for the now mythical Fox Software, and then as one of Bill Gates's minions at Microsoft. He is a husband, a father, a technophile and a movie buff.

If you'd like to get an e-mail alert whenever Kerry has a new book out or has a special on one of his already-released books, sign up at KerryNietz.com.

About DIGITAL DREAMS...

I don't have many short stories because most of my stories arrive as novels.

Size isn't something I plan, really. I get the niggle of an idea and typically it comes with a certain weight attached to it. And that weight usually translates to something the size of a novel. On very rare occasions I have a lighter idea, but I always tuck those away again to see if they'll gain some girth. They live only in the recesses of my mind.

The short stories that finally come to fruition do so because someone else shook them loose. On rare occasions, as is the case for this anthology's headliner, I write a story because I want to meet a specific personal challenge. As anyone who's heard of my *Peril in Plain Space* series doubtless suspects—I'm a sucker for a challenge.

So, for those who are interested, here are the circumstances that shook these stories loose.

Digital Dreams is the result of an odd and interesting personal challenge. My favorite cover artist, Kirk DouPonce, shared with me an unused cover that he'd originally created for another project. The image had two of my favorite things in it—space and robots. So, I asked Kirk if he'd allow me to use that cover if I wrote a story for it. He agreed and *Digital Dreams* is the result. The story is also the only one I've written seemingly set in the DarkTrench universe post-*Freeheads*. That universe will probably always be my cyber-playground of choice.

A Symphony of Words, along with half the stories here, is flash fiction, meaning that it had to be a thousand words or less (a useful size for periodical publication). It was written for the reboot of *Havok* magazine a few years ago. Head editor Andrew Winch asked me if I had something that could serve as their inaugural story for a season that had a "phoenix" theme. I'm pleased with how the story turned out, as it not only touches on the idea of rising from the ashes, but also, I think, speaks to the usefulness of science fiction writers. While most of communication today is hard-driving facts and opinions, the sci-fi writer says, "Just listen for a bit and I'll help you see."

The Little T-Rex is another Havok story, this time for an issue centered around dinosaurs. Editor Ben Wolf asked me to submit for the issue, but I didn't have any dino-centric ideas in my head. I had just started to learn about 3D printing, though, and had stumbled upon the idea of a printer that could print human tissue. I told Ben my strange idea—one that had nothing to do with prehistory—and he encouraged me to run with it. Sometime later, I was given the opportunity to review a consumer 3D printer. 3D printing has since become one of my favorite hobbies.

Hard's Watcher was originally published in the *Heroes of the Realm* anthology. It started out as a potential side story for my novel *Frayed*, but I set it aside because it didn't seem to fit the overall narrative of *Frayed*. Consequently, it languished in an abandoned folder of my computer until Becky Minor and Danielle Ackley-McPhail asked me to write a story for *Heroes*. I dusted the story off, figured out what it was about, and finished it. I'm grateful that Becky and Danielle nudged *Hard's Watcher* back into existence because I think it says something about misperceptions and our need to step beyond them.

The Extent is the result of an idea I'd had for a long, long time. I love astronomy. It was one of my favorite courses in college, and I still enjoy following the latest discoveries. No quicker way to feel small than to study a picture of the cosmos. It almost looks too pretty, doesn't it? Like a painted picture or a façade that someone might have constructed. No way to know until we go. *The Extent* was originally written for a sci-fi-only issue of Havok magazine, but it didn't make the cut and so was published online. It later became my first story to be published in a foreign magazine. (In Arabic, no less!)

Graxin is one of my oldest short stories now. It was originally published in the *Ether Ore* anthology for Marcher Lord Press and later found a home in *Mythic Orbits* by Bear Publications. I added it here for completeness and because I sort of like that crazy XV unit. (One of his cousins makes an appearance in my novel *Lost Bits*...if you're paying attention). I've always thought of *Graxin* as a twisted version of the "Pearl of Great Price" parable.

ThreadBare was originally published as flash fiction for Havok, but it didn't really want to be that short. The more I wrote about the main character, the more I wanted to write about him. So, crafting a story of under a thousand words proved difficult. To satisfy my urge to write more, I created a new series with ThreadBare as the hero, the first book of which is titled *Frayed*. If you like what you read here, I encourage you to check out those stories. This version of *ThreadBare* is slightly different than the one published in Havok. Author and publisher Travis Perry said the story could use a bit more resolution at the end. I agreed and this version is the result.

Secrets has been around for a while too. It represents the first story I wrote for the Takamo gaming universe. I've since written a novella and two novels in that universe, all of which I'm quite fond of. Takamo is a vast playground for a sci-fi author like me and the folks there are delightful to work with. They kindly gave me permission to include *Secrets* here. I hope it spurs readers to want to sample more of what Takamo has to offer, starting with *Rhats!*, of course.

Proteus was first published as part of a bound anthology that Havok created for its reboot. As one of the featured authors, I was given the opportunity to have a second story appear in that anthology (along with *A Symphony of Words*). The domain of *Graxin* had remained on my mind for some time, so I thought this was a great chance to go exploring there again. I almost gave up once—writing a story in 1000 words or less is always daunting—but Mr. Winch mercifully coaxed me through. I'm happy with how *Proteus* turned out. Glad to have it published here with its prequel.

There you have it. I hope you found these distractions enjoyable. I know I did.